*the leper*

# Sigmund Brouwer

# THE LEPER

*based on the painting by*
*Ron DiCianni*

Tyndale House Publishers, Inc., Wheaton, Illinois

Visit Tyndale's exciting Web site at www.tyndale.com

Designed by Dean H. Renninger

Edited by Curtis H. C. Lundgren

Published in association with the literary agency of Alive Communications, Inc., 7680 Goddard Street, Suite 200, Colorado Springs, CO 80920.

Scripture quotations are taken from the *Holy Bible,* King James Version.

Library of Congress Cataloging-in-Publication Data

Brouwer, Sigmund, date.
    The leper / by Sigmund Brouwer.
        p. cm.
ISBN 0-8423-4014-9 (hc : alk. paper)
1. Leprosy—Patients—Fiction.    I. Title.
PS3552.R6825 L47 2002
813'.54—dc21                                                              2002000251

Printed in the United States of America

07   06   05   04   03   02
6    5    4    3    2    1

*for Curtis*

Thanks always for wisdom, inspiration, and humor.

# prologue

THREE DAYS BEFORE CHRISTMAS, Nathaniel would abandon the woman who now waited for him onshore across the narrowing gap of water between the ship and the dock.

Suzanne did not know this, of course, and as Nathaniel's ship slowly docked at one of the wharves in the East End, her heart was filled with hope and anticipation. For three years, she had waited for Nathaniel to return.

She watched as crew members threw ropes as thick as a man's arm to dockworkers and continued to watch as, along the length of the ship, they tied the ropes in place to monstrous iron bars on the wharf. The plank was lowered, and within minutes a stream of men began to leave the ship. Each paused to look around in wonder and gratitude. This was home. Fair England. No matter that the buildings around them were grimed with centuries of soot, no matter that the sky was lead gray and the winter air forced them to shiver within their coats. This was home, a totally different world than India, with its wide blue skies over a parched hot land, filled with dark-skinned people who often refused to listen to their British overlords. The men stepping off the ship had endured three years of military service in the colony, then months of hazardous travel across the oceans. They were home!

Despite the winter chill, a sizable crowd of women and children waited to greet the men who stepped off the ship. The unmarried men—even with their minds on local pubs and entertainment, moral or not—watched with envy as first one woman, then another, peeled away from the group to hurry forward to a husband with cries of joy. Some of the women had young children who hung to their coats, shy children who were unsure what to think of the strange man embracing their mother.

The waiting crowd thinned as the ship continued to empty.

She, who was to be abandoned, held Faith, her daughter, in her arms. Her small son, Ethan, bravely stamped his feet and, for his mother's sake, valiantly pretended that the cold did not bother him.

She had blonde hair, pinned in place beneath a bonnet. The unlined skin of her face showed a complexion of uncommon fairness. Such was her beauty that many of the men—even the married ones with their arms around the waists of their wives—covertly and occasionally impudently tried to hold her glance. Her children reflected this attractiveness. The boy, who resembled much of his father, could be a dark-haired young prince. The four-year-old girl, curled asleep in her mother's arms, was exquisite.

The woman did not notice any of the admiring glances cast her way. She was focused on the return of her husband, whom she loved as fiercely as she loved her children.

Long after all the men had departed, she stared anxiously at the ship, unaware that Nathaniel, hidden from a vantage point between containers on the bow of the ship, watched her.

Finally, she gave up her vigil and sought a carriage that would return the three of them to their cottage in the West End.

Five minutes after she departed, Nathaniel made his way down the gangway to an empty plaza.

As Nathaniel walked through the gloomy late morning, passers-by could not see his face. Except for his eyes, it was covered with a scarf. He studied the street with each step, refusing to make eye contact, even with the painted women beckoning him from street corners, as if they expected him, like other newly arrived sailors in the area, to hurry into their arms.

It was not one of the painted women he wished to see, but a solicitor.

"AS LONG AS the information you have given is correct, it will not be difficult to arrange for your monthly military stipend to reach this office," the solicitor said an hour later. "Nor will it be difficult to disburse it according to your directions."

William Morgan, the solicitor, was on the verge of retirement. He was slightly balding, with the remainder of his gray hair clinging to his massive skull like a Roman warrior's helmet. His jowls reflected a life of success in the legal system as he sat behind his desk wearing a navy blue suit tailored to flow comfortably over his large belly. He held a quill and was prepared to jot down the most important points of this short-notice meeting with this client, who had secured this appointment by mentioning the family name of another respected client.

"The information is correct," said this client. "My directions are simple then. Divide it into two cashier's cheques. The bulk of it—nine-tenths—each month shall be sent in one cheque to my wife. The remainder each month to an address that will reach your office shortly."

"Until further notice?" William Morgan asked. He was curious about this client, who wore a long coat, a scarf covering most of his face, and gloves. He had not inquired but made a private, silent guess. The client spoke of a three-year stint in India. Most certainly, then, malaria with its horrible spells of shivering. *The poor man,* he guessed, *cannot stay warm.*

"There will be no further notice," William Morgan's client answered. "I doubt this great country of ours will ever forfeit on its payments to men of military service. That money will always reach you."

"Just so I understand." William Morgan scanned the notes on his desk and the information supplied. He repeated his client's instructions to redirect money to the woman. Repeated the address of the woman who would receive the bulk of the man's military pay. William Morgan did not ask the obvious question: why? Not after all these years of discretion as a solicitor.

"Yes, you are correct," the client said when William Morgan was finished speaking. "Furthermore, I will not return to this office. Ever. As long as my retirement pension is sent as directed."

"There will be a monthly fee," William Morgan said. *There is always a fee.*

"Certainly," the client answered. "I did not expect otherwise. Take it from my portion. Nothing must diminish her portion."

"Our business today is finished then?"

"Finished."

As a courtesy, William Morgan rose from behind his desk to escort his client to the doorway of his office. At the doorway, he extended a hand to this client.

Their eyes met briefly, and William Morgan, who, after all these years of representing clients caught in all sorts of legal matters, prided himself on the ability to judge a man's soul by the window of his eyes, was unable to determine exactly what state of mind this client had brought into his office and was taking back out again. Sorrow? Resignation? Resolution? Anger?

William Morgan's hand remained extended. After a moment of hesitation, the client accepted the handshake, but without removing the glove on his right hand.

William Morgan could not know it, of course, but this handshake would be the last physical contact his client would have with any human until the night, roughly four years later, that this client would stand on a wharf at the Thames and stare down on the water in preparation to end his own life.

AS THE SUN SET on that gloomy day shortly before Christmas, in a fashionable small cottage in London's West End, Suzanne stood on her doorstep and stared expectantly at a point where the road rose and disappeared over a slight hill. Other cottages, similar to the one in which she was raising her boy and girl, lined the road on both sides.

The boy was now five. Ethan. He was only a toddler when, three years earlier, his father stepped onto a ship bound for India. The girl, Faith, was nearly four. Month by month, this young mother had chronicled the growth of their two children in letters sent to the man she missed so badly. Month by month, she received letters of love and affection in return.

And now.

His ship had returned safely to London. She knew it, because she was there waiting when it arrived this morning. She had watched all the men leave. Surely she could not have missed seeing her husband among all of the passengers. Surely he could not have missed seeing her and the two children in the crowd as he passed by.

But that was her hope. Her only hope. She told herself that he could not have missed the ship's departure. Otherwise, it would be months more before his return on another ship. And, even though her mind tried to dwell on it during this long, long afternoon, she refused to think of any other explanation for this prolonged absence since the ship docked.

Bitter wind hit the doorway of her cottage. This young mother wrapped herself in a blanket to stay warm. She strained to see into the darkening gloom, for the sun, unseen behind the gray blanket of clouds, was within minutes of setting. She wanted to believe that at any moment her husband would appear at the top of the rise of the hill. With the children safely sleeping inside, she could not bear to pace as she waited for his return. She wanted to be able to rush forward and greet him.

Then . . .

The clattering of horses' hooves.

A hackney approached!

Yes, an outline of a carriage appeared on the rise. Made its way steadily downward toward the cottage. Stopped.

Had her husband, her beloved Nathaniel, arrived? Hope forced her heart to quicken as she rushed out of the cottage.

But a man did not get out.

Instead, the driver stepped down and walked toward her.

"Christmas greetings," he said, doffing his hat. "I've been instructed to deliver this."

He handed her an envelope with her name on the back.

Light that spilled from the cottage window showed her enough to recognize her husband's handwriting.

"Who gave this to you?" she demanded.

The driver shrugged. In his long coat, it was a movement hardly seen. "Some man. I saw nothing of his face. He said you'd pay once I delivered. Ten pence."

"Yes, of course," Suzanne said. Now dread filled her as surely as if the gray gloom about her had funneled into her soul. She stepped inside and returned with the money.

Another doff of the hat. Then the hackney clattered away, back over the rise.

But the woman did not see this. She reentered the cottage and removed the blanket that wrapped her body.

With her children asleep, she sat at a table that had been set for two with wineglasses and a meal prepared and waiting in the small oven.

She sat for long minutes, unmoving. The light of candles glowed against the beauty of her face. The envelope was in her hand.

She hardly dared open it, such was the strength of her sense of dread. Nathaniel had not returned. But a letter had arrived.

Finally, with shaking fingers, she opened the envelope. It contained a short letter in her husband's handwriting.

*Dear Suzanne,*
*There is no other way to say this. I have fallen in love with*
*another woman. So I will not return. I have taken care of our*

*family's financial needs, however. You will receive a monthly stipend through a barrister's office. His name is William Morgan and he can be reached at . . .*

The address of the solicitor blurred her vision as the tears began to fall.

She stood. In silence. She took a broom and began sweeping the floor, although it had been clean since she first prepared this evening's meal for her husband.

She continued to sweep with slow, mechanical movements.

The candles burned down to darkness.

Her children remained sleeping.

# 1

*Charing Cross, London*
*June 1853*

A LOUD CONTINUOUS SCREAM from the courtyard pierced the curtains and woke the Reverend Edward Terwillegar.

He was a middle-aged man and very unaccustomed to any excitement. This was by design. As a boy, Edward Terwillegar had loved listening to the stories about his brave ancestors and had for many years hoped he, too, might be equally brave. But through the sporting challenges inflicted upon him by a stern father, he discovered early— and with varying degrees of pain—that he did not have the quickness, constitution, or heart for challenges. Where some—like his younger brother—grew from testing, like steel forged in the face of fire, he,

Edward, slunk away from his various defeats. Until as a man, he found refuge far, far away from the manly pursuits of his generation.

It was something he freely admitted to himself, to the point that he actually believed it did not matter to him that he had never grown into the man of his father's vision.

Thus, when the screams woke him, he floundered upright in his bed and fought panic.

*Dear Lord*, he thought from his bedroom on the second floor of the manor, *it's happened. The archbishop was right in his pessimistic prediction. Someone from the Irish tenements has snuck onto the grounds and attacked one of the women of the monastery.*

The scream rose and fell and rose again.

In near total darkness, Reverend Terwillegar swung his legs out from his covers in haste and jumped forward, directly into his chamber pot. His feet skidded, spilling its contents. He fell backward and banged his hips into the side of his bed, then tumbled onto the floor.

The impact drove his breath from his lungs.

It took him several moments to recover. The screaming from the courtyard did not abate in the slightest. It gave him the motivation to roll over and push himself to his knees.

How he hated the cloudiness that seemed to overcome him in any crisis. That was one of the reasons he cherished being part of the clergy. Most of the problems he dealt with could be handled by leaning on clichés of comfort and by reading Scripture verses in a soothing voice.

*The lamp,* he told himself. *What is needed first is some light.*

In the dark, he fumbled for a match. It took him a panicky half minute to finally strike the head. With his free hand, he groped for his lamp and opened the glass cage.

The screaming in the background was a terrible distraction, and in his haste, Reverend Terwillegar pulled too hard on the cage door. It snapped off and fell from his fingers. Glass shattered on the floor.

*Calm, calm, calm,* he instructed himself.

Finally he managed to flame the wick. The lamp gave a satisfying glow, showing the plush furniture that had come with the estate. Reverend Terwillegar's cassock hung neatly from a hook on the inside of the door.

He studied the robe.

Stay in his nightclothes? Or change from his long gown? If any of the novices saw him straight from bed, it would be a tremendous breach of . . .

No, no. Some things were more important than propriety.

As a compromise, he reached for his nightcap and tugged it down to his ears.

Once again, he stepped forward. Pain pierced his big toe as he crunched the shattered glass. He bit back a howl and nearly dropped his lamp as he hopped on his good foot.

Not only had he forgotten the broken glass of the lamp, but the spilled contents of his chamber pot. He slipped on the unexpected wetness and again crashed backward, this time landing solidly on his hind end. The lamp crashed beside him, and as the oil spread, so did the flame that rode the top of it.

This new crisis sharpened him considerably. He rolled over onto his stomach, beating frantically at the flames. In seconds, he was in darkness again.

He exhaled relief. But his next indrawn breath reminded him that he had completely spread himself prone in the very wetness that had sent him tumbling.

And the screaming from outside did not relent.

Above that horrible noise, he heard loud rapping at his door. "Reverend Terwillegar! Reverend Terwillegar!"

"Yes," he answered to the sharp voice of Miss Hogg.

"Can't you hear that hideous screaming?"

"I hear it! I hear it!"

She rapped on the door again, as if he had not yet replied to her. "I'm waiting here. Must you dally like this?"

*Dear Lord,* he thought, *why this cross to bear? Any other woman but her as the one picked by the archbishop to . . .*

Instantly, he felt guilt. The screaming was indication enough of another person's dire problem, and here he was, dithering to complain about a vexation that a better man would be able to handle easily.

"Reverend Terwillegar!" The banging on the door grew fiercer. It would be no surprise, he thought, if a woman of her girth burst through the door itself. "Reverend Terwillegar!"

He found the strength to open the door to the large middle-aged woman he knew was on the other side.

Miss Ima Hogg stood with a lamp held high, throwing light across her broad shoulders. She was an awkward and unfashionable woman, with dark hair pinned into a severe bun. She wore a brown dress that hung from her in such a way that it gave her the appearance of a solid rectangular block with dull black shoes peeking from the bottom.

She also wore a deep frown.

How had she managed to pull herself together so quickly? Reverend Terwillegar wondered. More than likely, she'd been sitting by lamplight, studying Scripture so she could catch his mistakes during Sunday's sermon.

Ima sniffed the air, then lowered the light and raised it again, making no effort to hide the fact that she was inspecting the length of his tall body.

Reverend Terwillegar looked down. He saw blood leaking from the big toe of his right foot. His entire gown was darkened in a wide stain from the contents of the chamber pot. It was then he became aware of the sour odor that clung to him because of it.

Their eyes met and he saw her disapproval.

A tangle of gray hair fell from his forehead and in front of his vision. He pushed it back under his nightcap.

"Thank you for providing the light," he said with as much dignity as he could muster. "If you would be kind enough to hand me the lamp, I shall proceed. You may return to the women."

"Humph," she said. Without relinquishing the lamp, she marched toward the sound of the screaming.

He opened his mouth to remind her that he was the authority in all matters. But she was moving too quickly, and he felt ridiculous attempting to yell at her wide back.

Reverend Terwillegar followed. Until his next steps reminded him that his feet were still bare. He limped back into his room and found his slippers.

Then he chased after Miss Ima Hogg.

IMA HOGG.

Since childhood, all who heard it had laughed at hearing Ima's name, with sniggers that always seemed to reach her ears. As a tiny girl, she had not understood this laughter. As she grew older, however, no matter how nicely the maids dressed her for the parties at the mansions of her father's friends, she would endure those same sniggers at the endless parties where daintier and prettier girls danced with the partners she always lacked.

Ima Hogg.

The play on words in her name had been no accident. Bertrand Hogg, her father, was a determined shrewd brute who began as a laborer on the wharves near the Thames and fought and clawed hard enough and long enough to own a company with ten ships that ran coal from Newcastle down the North Sea and up the Thames to the city. With wealth, he did what all the newly wealthy of London did. Moved away from the slums and the filth and found a beautiful wife to serve all his needs. Including the urge for progeny. Bertrand Hogg had hoped his firstborn would be a son, but after years of waiting, the baby that finally arrived killed his wife in childbirth, and as further insult was no son but a squalling and ugly girl equipped with a harsh scream. In a drunken rage, Bertrand Hogg decided to punish her with the name that seemed so apt.

As a young woman, Ima stopped dreaming the dreams that other women her age held as tight as the bodices that helped them form pretty figures while hers remained uncurved. In the age of Victoria, women mattered only for their looks and interesting conversation and ability to deliver healthy boys. Ima realized early there was no point in bruising her heart by slamming it against the unyielding reality of what nature had not given her. As she grew older, she refused to become the sort of spinster who set lonely tables for two and ate by candlelight immersed in warm fantasy.

In adulthood, as London grew and slums encroached upon the family mansion, Ima's consolation became the Church of England, with its strictly defined parameters of right and wrong that promised the justice she had not been given with birth. There, too, the sniggers were hidden better, for within the church, appearances of nicety mattered more than without.

Yet often the refuge of the church felt like a prison. Just as Ima had been cursed with a close resemblance to her father, she had also been cursed with his fierce competitive drive. In 1853, women did not lead the Church of England; they were its servants.

When Bertrand died of cholera a few years earlier, Ima had final revenge on her hateful father, for much as he had tried later for a son with different wives, she was his sole heir. Miss Hogg donated her father's estate grounds to the church, on the condition that the grounds were used solely to found a commune for women dedicated to serving the Christ. Since Henry VI—four centuries earlier—all monasteries had been banned in England. But two years before, Queen Victoria had finally permitted one to be formed for men. When Ima approached the archbishop of Canterbury, he could see no reason to refuse the pioneering effort of one for women, especially in light of the gift to the church offered by Ima. The suffrage movement was gaining momentum, and this would nicely give the Church of England a modern respectability, without costing it any power. More importantly, the archbishop had a good sense of real estate, and with London growing so quickly as an industrial and financial center, he knew the future worth of the estate once it passed into the church coffers on Ima's death. Most importantly, he was a man of compassion and felt it could help women who wanted to dedicate their lives to meaningful worship.

For Ima, it seemed she had found a place of relative contentment for the rest of her life. Except for the necessity of dealing with Reverend Edward Terwillegar—the inept clergyman who oversaw the commune because even the archbishop could not allow it to appear that a woman was actually in power—Ima believed she was happy with the prospect of years of quiet, dedicated service to the Christ and her reward beyond.

Screaming, however, was not civilized. Nor did it belong on her grounds, day or night.

And she intended to do something about it.

AS THE ESTATE GROUNDS and its twenty-three women were near the Irish tenements with all the trouble promised by a combination of underpaid labor and cheap ale, an elderly watchman named John Cappe had been hired to walk the grounds during the night and keep the lamps supplied with oil.

Ever conscious of his diminutive stature and timid nature mocked constantly by acquaintances at the Pig & Kettle, John Cappe had earlier armed himself—as he did for each of his nightly vigils of the parish grounds—with swigs of gin and his massive dog—dark, broad shouldered, and waist high to any man—usually at the end of a taut leash.

Fear was the reason John Cappe had raised his massive dog as if it were his child. Fear. Bad enough walking the streets during the day, anticipating terror around every alley corner until he reached the sanctuary of the Pig & Kettle. He always dreaded nights, and sleeping with his dog gave him badly needed reassurance through the dark hours.

It was the desperation for easy money that had led him to

accept employment on the grounds, among the shadows of the trees on clear, moonlit nights, or worse, when fog descended and shrieks and wails from the tenements carried to the grounds like cries from the devil.

Despite his fear of the dark, the lack of exertion was perfect employment for a man of John Cappe's age, and certainly a way to compensate for all the years he had sacrificed to find the food to sustain such a large dog. Each night, the cheap gin helped conquer some of his fears, and he limited his rounds of walking in the frightful night, choosing to sleep as much as possible in the doorway of the new church building in the center of the grounds.

In that hour before dawn, the bullmastiff had began to growl, waking John Cappe in the doorway.

Since his first night on the grounds, John Cappe had dreaded a moment such as this.

"Easy, boy," he whispered. "Steady now. No reason to panic."

He decided if he called out, the intruder—or more terrifying, the intruders—would flee and there would be no reason for confrontation.

Yet as John Cappe had tried to croak out a shout, fear choked his throat, and he was able to expel only a feeble gasp instantly lost in the thick dark fog beyond the church entrance. Before he could make another attempt to shout warning, his dog had risen and rushed forward. The leash at the end of his wrist had pulled John Cappe upward and forward into the swirling fog of the courtyard.

Five minutes later, the screaming had begun.

His.

# 2

AS IMA HOGG and the reverend approached the source of the screams, the outer edge of her lamp's circle of light first showed small John Cappe, tugging at the leash of his dog. Their next steps brought the sight of the crouched dog, holding firm the end of a leg. And then, with one more step, the owner of that firmly held leg, a hooded intruder, lying back in a shrub, blanketed bundle in arms.

It wasn't the intruder who screamed, but poor John Cappe, transfixed with horror by the sight of his dog passionately engaged in the task it had been bred to fulfill.

John Cappe's voice lost no volume at the approach of Ima Hogg and the clergyman.

Ima handed the lamp to Reverend Terwillegar.

"Shut that gob of yours," Ima said, astonishing Reverend Terwillegar with her use of the vernacular. Without hesitation she smacked the watchman across his head, and he snapped his mouth shut in midscream.

Using just one arm, she swept the watchman aside. And Ima began to fiercely kick the dog. Finally it let go.

She kicked it twice more until it backed away. It made one tentative move back toward the fallen intruder, and she landed another mighty kick on its ribs, the solid thump seeming to echo briefly.

The dog whimpered.

John Cappe began to protest. "Go easy on 'im. No need for such—"

"Back to your gin," she snarled. The reverend might be blind to the watchman's failings, but she was not. "You've done your job. Including the dreadful panic you've spread among all the women here with that screaming of yours. What nonsense. We'll discuss it in the morning, and you'll be fortunate to retain employment here."

"I say, Miss Hogg," Reverend Terwillegar said from behind the lamp. "Perhaps that's a matter of authority that is something for me to decide at my con—"

"I doubt this is the time to argue," she snapped. There was no other way to think of this man; he was a ditherer, afraid of offending anyone, and in so doing, pleased no one. That's what she hated about the world of men. Politics and connections, not qualifications, gave men positions they did not deserve. "It's well past midnight, and we have an intruder in our midst. Shouldn't you be fetching a bobby?"

She turned on the watchman, who was mesmerized by her fierceness. "And why haven't you gone and taken that cur with you?"

Watchman and dog meekly departed, leaving the circle of light and disappearing into the darkness beyond.

That's when Ima heard the quiet crying of the baby in the intruder's arms.

UNTIL THIS MOMENT, Nathaniel thought he understood the depths of pain and sorrow that a human heart could endure. Now, with these events beyond his control, with the large angry woman bending toward him, he could not turn back from his decision, even if he wanted. And he had never felt more broken.

Perhaps it was just as well. He did not know if, in the end, he would have had the courage to walk away from the church doorstep and leave the baby behind.

"Get up, you," the woman said to him. "If you've brought us a slum child, this is not the place for a foundling. We've charity hospitals for the likes of you." She grabbed his arm and hauled him upward from the shrub.

Nathaniel stumbled to keep his balance. There was no pain from his ankle. Nor had he expected any. Little Gabrielle shifted in his arms, and he clung to her as fiercely as she clung to him.

"Speak up," the woman demanded. "Was that your intent? To leave a foundling on the steps? If so, I expect God inflicted that dog upon you as punishment. And as further punishment if you're an unmarried woman too foolish to avoid sin. If so, we'll be glad to help our Holy Father. For we'll not be sending you off with a penny or two and a loaf of bread. No, it's high time irresponsible mothers like you were stopped. And a judge will make a fine example of you."

"Miss Hogg," Reverend Terwillegar said. Nathaniel recognized that voice. "Perhaps you might think in a more charitable way. Let's tend to this woman's wounds. See to the baby. In the light of day, then, we'll see about punishment."

"No." Nathaniel spoke barely above a whisper. He'd made a mistake. This was not the place where Gabrielle should be raised. He'd hoped for mercy from the Reverend Edward Terwillegar, and he'd pinned an envelope with money and a note requesting that. Far better here, he'd thought earlier, than a foundling hospital, where Gabrielle would be apprenticed barely a few years after she'd learned to walk. But if this fierce, horrible woman was in charge, he wanted Gabrielle to have no part of it. "Let me go. I shall take her elsewhere."

"Your ankle," Reverend Terwillegar said. "Surely—"

"Surely nothing, Reverend," the large woman interrupted harshly. "She condemns herself. She did intend to leave the baby. And I intend to see her punished. Just as I intend to make sure this baby is removed from such a negligent mother and sent to a hospital."

The large woman reached for Gabrielle.

Nathaniel tried to pull back.

The woman was too quick and too strong. She held the baby tight. Briefly, they each tugged at Gabrielle. But instantly her soft cries became a wail. Nathaniel let go, worried that Gabrielle might get hurt.

Nathaniel felt the baby's arms slide away from his neck. And with it, he felt as if the earth had opened up below him to swallow him into blackness. All these days, trying to find the strength to do this, he had bottled his sorrow, trying not to think beyond the moment when Gabrielle would be out of his life forever.

Now she was away. Her pitiful cry for his comfort broke the dam that had held back all that sorrow. He fell to his knees, unable in sudden weakness even to sob. He barely heard the woman's voice in his ears.

"Get up," she was saying. "Get up. You should have thought all of this through before you decided to abandon your baby."

Dimly, he was aware that she had moved to stand over him.

Dimly, he was aware that she reached for his hood.

Had he not been so broken in spirit, he would have twisted away, for the one single thing that he had to do to protect Gabrielle was ensure that no one saw his face.

But it was too late.

The woman yanked back his hood.

And this time, it was the reverend who screamed at the hole in the center of the man's face.

A FEW HOURS LATER, the sun began to rise. Already, the steam trains began to move along the tracks, blowing dark high columns of soot. Although the estate grounds were easily a mile away, the soot drifted overhead on a languid breeze of a rare hot clear morning.

Most of the women were still on their knees for early morning prayers, and the steam whistles were a familiar interruption to them. But not to Nathaniel, lying on straw in a stone shed already beginning to fill with heat.

Unlike many of the buildings on the estate grounds, the stone shed had been there for centuries, its walls smoothed by long exposure to rain and fog and cold. Once it had been used as a place to slaughter animals. The stench of blood had long faded, and later, it had become a holding pen for calves, and over the years, when empty, a romantic meeting place for the servants of the estate. Now, except for Nathaniel, the shed was nearly empty. Only straw on a dirt floor and the hard, bare stone walls.

He was alone. Without Gabrielle.

The baby had been securely quarantined in an attic.

GABRIELLE. Wide, round blue eyes. Blonde, wispy hair. A fine row of top teeth. The baby had two bottom teeth already through her gums and was getting two more on the top. Not yet a year old.

She was accustomed to solitude and had learned to amuse herself by clutching at her toes when she lay on her back, gurgling softly with contentment. By nature, she was happy and complained little, unless hungry to the point of pain in her stomach. The man who found her had rarely let that happen, and during much of her waking moments, Gabrielle smiled and cooed and slapped her hands up and down with joy.

Alone now, she was puzzled. Not afraid. Usually, her solitude occurred in darkness, when Nathaniel was gone. Now it was light; and without fail, he had always returned to her by then.

And usually her darkness was lively, filled with music and

shouting that rose from the pub below. Now, although the strange sound of the steam whistle woke her, Gabrielle was trying to comprehend this new sound. Silence.

Gabrielle explored this silence by speaking into it, using words that were hardly more than nonsense syllables.

She rolled over. Squirmed onto her knees. Braced against the wall and pushed to her feet to stand against it. This she had learned only days earlier. How to see the world from a higher vantage point.

She turned her head to peer up at the early sunlight that came through a tiny window of the attic. She lost her balance briefly and tottered away from the wall. Instinctive muscle movements steadied her.

Gabrielle didn't realize it immediately, but she was walking. Without support. For the first time. With no one to witness.

Seconds later, she did understand that something new had happened to her body. Something exciting. And when her conscious mind turned toward the fact that she was standing, it frightened her slightly, and she clunked down on her behind, seeking the safety of what she knew.

Crawling.

Gabrielle rustled across the floor.

A rumble in her little belly reminded her that she was hungry.

She called. Not a wail, for she was not angry. But an exploratory cry. She had learned that it only took that cry for the man who loved her to appear and hold her and feed her and sing to her.

This time, however, no one answered.

3

BEFORE GABRIELLE HAD ENTERED NATHANIEL'S LIFE, he
had lived alone in a rented room above a pub, where over the years
he had learned to ignore the songs and the drunken shrieks. He had
learned to live with the irony that only a thin floor separated him
from all that he could not have—contact with humans.

It was a simple arrangement with the owner of the pub. Follow-
ing his visit to the barrister's office, Nathaniel had first presented
himself to the pub owner in the same manner he had appeared to
William Morgan, his face hidden by scarves and his hands in gloves.
Unlike his visit to the barrister, however, Nathaniel had offered an
excuse, telling the owner that he had been badly disfigured in a fire
and wished to live in total privacy.

From that day on, by arrangement, each morning and evening

the wife of the pub owner set a meal in front of the door and
knocked twice before departing. Each morning and evening
Nathaniel waited until the footsteps had disappeared before opening the door and snatching the food inside. Immediately upon
finishing his food, he set the dishes outside and later heard the
woman retrieve them.

Nathaniel's only distractions during the day were reading
and writing. He dared not venture forth. Enough sunlight filtered
through a small, grime-crusted window to give him the needed
light. With his morning meal came one of the dailies, and once a
week he permitted himself the luxury of a used book, delivered
by the pub owner in the same way the meals arrived.

The pub owner was ignorant and rarely managed to bring the
book that Nathaniel requested through the notes he used to communicate with the man. That mattered little to Nathaniel. At least he
was able to read something.

Often, however, he set aside his book and returned to a small
stack of letters. These he carefully kept in chronological order. These
were the letters written to him by his wife during his time away in
India. He had read through the letters so often that he had them
memorized. But he did not read them for the surprises. Instead, he
lingered over each sentence, letting the words and her dainty handwriting trigger memories of times they shared.

He read her letters daily, and each day wrote new ones to her
that he would never post; these conversations were as close as he
could get to her.

But then there were the hours late at night when the songs
and the drunken shrieks ended. When the scraping of barstools
against the floor told him that the owner and his wife were

sweeping the floors and setting the stools upside down on the tables of the pub.

It was this silence that always woke Nathaniel.

And the silence that sent him into the night. Fully cloaked. With no one on the streets to see what damage leprosy had begun to inflict upon his body.

EACH NIGHT DURING THOSE YEARS after writing a letter to Suzanne he traveled a short distance from the pub, through the shadows and darkness to the fashionable small cottage in London's West End that held his sleeping family. There was a spot between trees where he could remain until dawn threatened to expose him with the day's first light. From there, each night he watched the cottage for any danger that might come upon it. An intruder. The smoke or flames that might signal a fire.

This was his family, and he would protect them in the only way that was possible for him. Rain, fog, sleet. No bad weather kept him from this nightly duty. It was his reason for existence.

Each night, as he stood among the trees, he tried not to think about Suzanne and Ethan and Faith, about how they slept so near yet so far out of his reach.

He simply watched.

Then as dawn approached, he would return to the room above the pub.

Except for Saturday nights.

DURING THE HOUR before dawn on every Sabbath, Nathaniel left the trees where he guarded the cottage and hurried another half mile to an abandoned match factory that overlooked a small church.

Because once earlier he had broken the lock, it was a simple task, pulling the lock open and slipping inside the rickety structure.

He climbed crooked stairs in the darkness, wondering each time if this was the occasion they would collapse beneath his weight. He found his vantage point near a broken window. There, before each Sabbath, he settled in and waited for dawn.

As church bells gonged the hour, dozens of worshipers would crowd the entrance to the church. Unlike the much more prosperous Westminster Abbey, there was no line of horse-drawn carriages to add to the festive feeling of a gathering of people.

Still, it was with no difficulty that Nathaniel, from his perch in the upper floor of the match factory, could pick out his family among all the others below. Suzanne, he would think fondly, was a creature of habit, and their arrival time did not vary by one minute from week to week. As always, she would hold Ethan's hand in her left and Faith's hand in her right.

It always bothered Nathaniel that Suzanne wore the same dress she had been wearing to church for the last two years. The same hat. The same gloves. Were that his monthly stipend would allow her more luxuries.

As for the boy and the girl . . .

Suzanne took care to ensure that they were dressed neatly if not richly. Ethan's hair was dark, like Nathaniel's. Faith had the light blonde hair of her mother. Ethan's britches were always too short and looked painfully tight. Faith's dresses were brightly colored; Nathaniel had no doubt Suzanne sewed them from material taken from cheap used clothing.

It seemed to Nathaniel that he was able to see the growth in his children from week to week. It was an absurd thought, he knew, for Ethan was seven years old now and Faith nearly six. That was long past the startling quickness from which they go from teething and crawling to fully weaned and walking.

As he was a man of logic, Nathaniel also told himself that his upper perch was too far away for his vision to fully appreciate any subtle changes from the week before. Thus, he reminded himself, he was only thinking wishfully as he noted their progress from week to week.

Always, this glimpse of his family would be too brief. When the church bells fell to silence, Suzanne marched Ethan and Faith inside without hesitation. This meant Nathaniel would have at least two hours of solitude until he saw them again for a few precious minutes after the church service was finished. And then he faced the long wait through the day until darkness allowed him to venture back to the room above the pub.

It was not much.

But it was something.

And he knew he would continue these vigils each Sabbath until he saw what he needed to see. Only then would he finally permit himself to say good-bye to his family.

# 4

AFTER THE EARLY MORNING devotion service to the Christ, Miss Hogg departed quickly from the sanctuary to prepare for her next task.

She retreated into a room in the manor at the opposite end of Reverend Terwillegar's living quarters. The sun had risen an hour earlier, and strong rays passed through the curtained window onto lacquered antiques.

As she wrapped her face with the expensive linen strips that she intended to burn after they had been contaminated, Miss Hogg did not use a mirror to assist herself; among the knickknacks and doilies and expensive gleaming walnut furniture and three clocks of varying sizes, there was no mirror.

Neither was there a tray with powders or blushes to flatter her complexion. Having long ago accepted her ugliness, she had stopped making any effort to disguise it. To prove even further that she now cared little about her appearance, she cut her own hair to hang flat and straight edged on her forehead, accentuating the squareness of her sullen face.

She covered all of her face except her eyes. She moved on to wrap her hands with the strips of expensive linen.

Just as she finished there was a knock on her door—as expected. She glanced at the clock to confirm her punctuality. And, of course, her visitor's. Reverend Terwillegar might be her superior in title but certainly not in fact.

Beneath the linen strips, she pursed her lips.

The reverend had arrived almost two minutes late.

"DID YOU BURN THE WHEELBARROW?" Ima Hogg's muffled voice reached Reverend Terwillegar directly outside her door. He carried a bottle of warm milk in one hand and a bowl of porridge in the other.

Although sunlight filled the hallway, Reverend Terwillegar fought a yawn brought on by fatigue. He had not had any sleep since the scream woke him hours earlier.

"Yes, I burned it." Reverend Terwillegar held the small bottle and some clean rags. He felt ridiculous talking to the door. "A perfectly good wheelbarrow. At dawn as you instructed, so the flames wouldn't draw attention. Even then it wasn't early enough. Some of the women were on their way to prayers. The curious eyebrows it raised was enough to—"

"Did you tell anyone why?"

"Did I tell anyone why?" Reverend Terwillegar wanted sleep. He wanted his routine returned to him. Mostly, he wanted this dreadful problem gone. A leper and a foundling hidden within the parish grounds! It had been years since anything had given him cause to be upset—except, of course, for the archbishop's decision to start this women's commune—and he found himself filled with an unfamiliar emotion. Irritation. Especially since Ima Hogg had seemed to take entire control of all of this. Or was he irritated that she seemed much more capable than he?

Words that surprised him began to come out of his mouth. "Did I tell anyone why I was burning a wheelbarrow instead of leading the women in service? Yes. I stopped each one of them and told them we had found a leper in a dead faint and had used the wheelbarrow to carry him to a place where we could lock him up. I told them I was so deathly afraid that this disease might spread that I was burning anything he had contacted. Then, of course, I felt it necessary to tell them about the baby, which you have taken hostage and—"

Ima's muffled voice stopped him again. "If you are developing a sense of humor, Reverend, this is the most inappropriate time for it that I can imagine."

Perhaps Reverend Terwillegar was emboldened by the door between him and the intimidating woman on the other side. "Oh, for heaven's sakes, Miss Hogg, you're making entirely too much of this. As for burning every single thing that might have come in contact with him, I'll let you know that was a perfectly good bed gown and—"

Reverend Terwillegar stepped back as the door opened. He took a step back at the apparition that stood in the doorway. "M-Miss Hogg?"

The large creature in front of him had rags wrapped around its hands and face, with dark holes for the eyes to look forth. Reverend Terwillegar immediately thought of Egyptian mummies, like those that had been among the artifacts that had been displayed recently in the museum.

"As I said," she warned, "this is not an appropriate time for any humor."

"Miss Hogg, is all of this entirely necessary?"

"I am tired of arguing with you," she said.

"Arguing? I've done nothing all night through except jump at your every command."

"See? There you are. At it again. You ask me if this is necessary? It has been centuries since monasteries have been permitted here in England. Even more revolutionary is the fact that the archbishop recognizes the importance of woman's suffrage and has allowed me to pioneer this women's commune. If anything goes wrong, I let down all women across this nation. Do you understand?"

Reverend Terwillegar found himself fascinated by words coming from a mouthless head that bobbed in animated anger.

"Do you understand?" she repeated.

"Ahem. Yes."

"And if we send the leper back in their midst and the public finds out, how long do you think our small organization would be permitted to exist after showing such irresponsibility?"

"Miss Hogg, we discussed this thoroughly last night, and I was in total agreement to let the archbishop make the final decision."

"Ha!"

Reverend Terwillegar jumped. "Ha?"

"Ha! My point exactly."

A strip of rag started to uncurl from Ima Hogg's head. Reverend Terwillegar wondered what the etiquette was in this sort of situation. Ignore it? Point it out? Reach forward and tuck it back in place?

Ima Hogg shook a rag-covered hand at him. "I need to write the letter, which I shall send by messenger. At best, it will reach him by noon. If we are fortunate, we may receive a return letter by tomorrow or even the next day after."

"Tomorrow? Certainly he can send a message by carriage, as we did for him. How long will it take for him to make a decision?"

Without waiting for him, Miss Hogg began to walk down the hallway toward the stairs that led to the attic.

He found himself striding rapidly to keep up. Warm milk splashed out of the bottle onto his dark clothes. Some porridge oozed onto his fingers.

"Why should he hurry it?" Miss Hogg asked over her shoulder. "He'll know from our letter that we've sworn to keep the leper's presence a secret from the public. He's our problem until the archbishop decides to make it his. And, man of God that he is, he's no political fool. What if we keep the leper for weeks?"

"Weeks?" Reverend Terwillegar echoed. This *was* dreadful. To make it even worse, there was the note he had found earlier with the baby's shawl. A note addressed directly to him. It was definitely not something he would mention to Miss Hogg; she gloried in any perceived advantage, and if she believed that Edward was in any way responsible for the arrival of the baby, his life would become infinitely more unbearable.

29

"Weeks," Miss Hogg declared. "In the meantime, who will feed the baby?"

"Well, I . . ."

"My point exactly," she repeated. "You hadn't thought of it."

He had not. The note had taken his full attention and had already caused him hours of worry.

"I've already decided it must be me," Miss Hogg continued, "much as I dread the prospect. I'm the one to have touched the leper. I'm the only one in danger. No sense endangering anyone else by contamination. The success of this commune means everything to me, and I'll make every necessary sacrifice for it."

"But I'm the one delivering food to the leper," Reverend Terwillegar said.

"By pushing it into his shed with a pole. Much as I would like to do the same for the baby, I will have to go in there and ensure she is healthy."

"Let the leper feed the baby. They've already been in contact with each other." Even as he said it, Reverend Terwillegar felt foolish. If the baby had not contracted the disease yet, it was unfair to continue to expose the baby to the danger again and again.

Miss Hogg stopped so abruptly that Reverend Terwillegar almost slammed into her broad body. She spun and faced him, giving him that eerie view of her masked face.

"You know all the sentimental nonsense that people have toward babies," Miss Hogg stormed from behind her mask. "If word of keeping them together leaks to the public, we'll be vilified just as badly as if we'd let the leper back on the streets."

"Yes, yes," Reverend Terwillegar said. "Your arguments are unassailable."

"Of course they are, Reverend Terwillegar; I have given this much thought. I am right, and this is the right course of action. Therefore, we must take it."

She began to walk again and quickly climbed the stairs to the attic.

"And what will we tell the others here?" Reverend Terwillegar called up to her from the bottom of the short stairs. "We can't go on like this for days and days until the archbishop replies."

She waited for him to reach the door to the attic before she spoke. "Tell them the truth," she snapped. "Now that we have the baby and the leper in isolation, and now that I cannot contaminate anyone, there is no need for panic."

Reverend Terwillegar found himself nibbling his lower lip.

"And, Reverend, stop doing that with your lip. You do it every time you're at a loss. It does not inspire confidence."

Reverend Terwillegar could hardly believe that a large mummy was so directing him. Even if it was Ima Hogg, who had increasingly taken over the parish.

"Confidence? Miss Hogg, I am a clergyman, not a soldier."

Behind her, the baby began to cry at the sound of voices outside the attic.

Miss Hogg banged the door several times. "Hush," she commanded.

She turned back to Reverend Terwillegar. "Let's be plain, here, Reverend. You don't like me. And I don't like you. No sense hiding that while we have this crisis to deal with. But I don't care whether you like me, because I have my duties and they are far more important than my popularity. Think on that while you waffle back and forth, trying to please everybody. I truly believe you are in the clergy because it is the only place for a man to be meek and mousy without anyone laughing to his face. This is no time for you to hide behind your collar."

Reverend Terwillegar lifted a hand to begin a weak protest.

Ima Hogg ignored him and grabbed the bottle of milk. She opened the door to face the growing wails of the baby.

"That's enough of that," she said to the baby. "You'll learn soon enough my way."

She slammed the door behind her as she entered, leaving Reverend Terwillegar alone at the top of the stairs.

# 5

STRIPED BY THE SHADOWS from the meager sunlight that fell
through the cracks of the old masonry, Nathaniel sat with his back
propped against the stone wall of the interior of the shed.

He cursed his stupidity and weakness. Somewhere, his poor
Gabrielle needed him. He imagined her cries of loneliness, and they
rang through his mind like instruments of torture.

His only consolation was the certainty that Reverend Edward
Terwillegar would now be forced to honor the request Nathaniel
had included in the letter pinned to Gabrielle's shawl. For that
reason, Nathaniel expected that any moment would bring the
arrival of Reverend Terwillegar.

That had not been his plan. Nor the reason for the letter.
Nathaniel had fully intended to be able to slip onto the grounds

and leave Gabrielle to be found, hoping the letter would protect her, hoping the Reverend Edward Terwillegar would take her in and raise her because of the letter.

Nathaniel, however, had not expected the large dog or the night watchman. Nor that he would be caught and imprisoned here. And certainly not that his leprosy would be discovered. With all the shrieking about a baby contaminated by the disease.

There was a silver lining in this dark cloud, for now Nathaniel's hope was almost a certainty. Now Nathaniel would be able to present his plea in person. Edward would not be able to refuse it then.

For it was not coincidence that had led Nathaniel to this place.

But the knowledge that of any men in this world, he might place Gabrielle into the mercy of the man in authority here.

Edward Terwillegar.

Nathaniel's brother.

WHEN MISS HOGG opened the door of the small attic, curiosity temporarily stopped Gabrielle's small cries of hunger. She had been standing along one wall, holding herself steady with one hand and running her other hand over the patterns of the wallpaper, using the distraction of this sensation to dull the pains that pinched her tiny stomach.

"Bah?" Gabrielle asked, still balanced along the far wall but half turned to peer over her shoulder.

Face and hands wrapped in white linen strips, Ima stepped inside with a bowl of lukewarm porridge.

"Bah!" Gabrielle was excited to have company. She dropped to her knees and scrambled toward her visitor. In her excitement, she tried to crawl too fast, and her arms gave way. She fell onto her head, immediately pushed up again, and hurried toward her visitor.

When she reached Ima, she pulled herself up on Ima's skirt and peered upward, standing on little feet. Who was this person in white?

"Bah?" Gabrielle asked. A small piece of dirt clung to Gabrielle's forehead from when she had fallen in her haste to greet the visitor.

"Humph," Ima replied. The baby blocked her forward progress. Even though her hands were safely wrapped in linen, she wanted as little contact with the baby as possible. So she shook her legs to knock the baby's grip loose, until the baby fell backward and landed on its small behind.

"Bah?"

"Humph."

Ima stepped farther inside the attic and set the bowl of porridge down on the floor. She stepped away. The energy in the baby showed perfect health. For now. Ima did not know how long it took to discover the symptoms of leprosy, but that would be answered soon enough. "There's enough to feed three of you. Be done with it."

Gabrielle spun toward it and gleefully plunged both her hands in the porridge.

"No!" Ima said. "You have a spoon!"

Which Gabrielle took and splashed into the porridge, then slapped onto the floor.

"No!" Ima said. "You ill-mannered urchin. Eat! That's all you get. I'm warning you. Waste not, want not."

Reverend Terwillegar stood in the doorway. He coughed discreetly. "I believe," he said, "a child this young must be fed."

While not a father, he had two sisters, each with three children. During his Sunday afternoon visits to their respective households, he had observed much of what it took to raise babies.

"Feed her. But that would mean—"

"Yes," he said, guessing correctly Ima's protest. "You'll have to hold her and spoon the porridge into her mouth."

This was not something Ima had expected. An only child, raised by a nanny, then friendless into spinsterhood, she'd never been around children or around any women who had children.

Gabrielle happily dumped the bowl over and then rubbed her hands in the mess on the straw.

"Now we need another bowl," Ima complained. "I really did not expect to have to make another trip to the kitchen and back. I have so much to do today. There's that letter to the archbishop, a discussion with the slovenly night watchman, my prayer time, my devotions to read. This street urchin is going to take me away from so much worship. . . ."

"Another bowl of porridge," Reverend Terwillegar repeated, "and your return with some cloths to clean the poor thing. If my nose serves me correctly, she has, um, defecated."

"In her clothing?" To Ima, this was not part of the noble mantle of martyrdom that she had assumed by insisting she be the one to look after the leper baby until the archbishop made his decision. "In her clothing? How vulgar."

"In her clothing," Reverend Terwillegar said, secretly happy to finally see Ima on the verge of defeat, even one this minor. "Babies do this frequently. I expect you'll have to tend to her every few hours."

"Every few hours? I'll do no such thing!"

"Then who will? After all, you made it very clear that we wanted to keep the risk of spreading leprosy to an absolute minimum."

"But defecation?" Underneath the white linen strips that covered her face, Ima felt the warmth of a blush. *Defecation.* Such matters to discuss. She was glad that the linens covered her nose. To actually smell the defecation of another human being! And what if some of it contacted her hands or clothing?

"She'll be hungry just as often." Reverend Terwillegar could not help his sense of triumph. "In one end and out the other. Again and again and again. Worse than any goose, I can assure you."

"That will be quite enough," Ima said, finally understanding that Reverend Terwillegar enjoyed her apparent helplessness. She would not give him the satisfaction. "I'll feed this baby and clean it as often as necessary."

Her mind briefly went to the number of linen strips it would take to cover herself anew each few hours. Should she not insist on burning it and instead reuse it? No, she decided without hesitation. The expense of new linen was little against the risk of catching leprosy from the baby.

"Bah? Bah? Bah?"

Ima had not noticed the baby reach upward for her. She looked down to see the baby's porridge-filled fingers grasp her skirt, spreading the porridge in clumps.

"No!" Ima shuffled backward until the baby fell away. "Now I'll have to clean my skirt!"

"Bah," Gabrielle said.

"Bah, yourself," Ima said. She fumed as she marched toward the doorway. "Learn to say something else."

Reverend Terwillegar was slow to move from the doorway.

"Out of my way," she snarled.

Gabrielle saw the door begin to close as they both left. She began to howl. Her cries clearly reached Ima and Reverend Terwillegar on the other side.

Ima glared at Reverend Terwillegar, but all of the effect was lost because of the linens that wrapped her face. "Look what you've done," she accused him. "I suppose she'll make that horrible noise all the day long."

"No," he said, hiding his smile. "I expect once she sees you again with a bowl of porridge, she'll be much happier. And even happier once you get her little bottom clean."

"Bah," Ima said. She marched down the steps toward the kitchen, with a few strips of loose linen trailing from her arms.

# 6

THE SLIDING OF AN EXTERIOR BOLT alerted Nathaniel to his visitor. He pulled his cloak over his head and sat as straight as his strength allowed him.

When the door opened, Nathaniel blinked against the brightness from inside the shadows of his hood, seeing only the outline of the man in the doorway. One hand was at the man's side. The other hand held the letter that had earlier been pinned to Gabrielle's shawl.

Nathaniel held himself very still, afraid if he stirred in any way at all, the dam would burst, that his body would betray him with sobs of relief and dread. He knew the letter would reach Edward, and he had been expecting his brother to arrive any moment.

Finally, the truth had come out.

"Please stay where you are and keep your distance," Reverend

Terwillegar said, remaining in the doorway. "I'm sure you understand why. Your condition is not something we want to be responsible for spreading to others."

"Of course," Nathaniel said. Even to himself, his strained voice
sounded like that of a stranger. How long had it been since he spoke
to anyone except Gabrielle, and that only in whispers and croons?

"You have tended to your ankle, I presume," said Edward.

"I found the food when I woke. And the bandages." Nathaniel
was disappointed in Edward's restraint. He hadn't expected a reunion
of tearful embrace, but at least some sort of surprise. Sorrow at
Nathaniel's leprosy, joy at finding him again, comprehension at
why Nathaniel had disappeared from their world. "I wrapped my
ankle as best I could."

"Good, good. Again, you'll understand our hesitation. Your
condition—"

Nathaniel could not help an interruption. He'd always been the
more passionate of the two, Edward almost priggish. "Call it leprosy,"
Nathaniel snapped. "Merely speaking of it won't contaminate you."
He immediately regretted his outburst. If he were in Edward's position, might he not react the same?

"Yes, of course." Edward had not moved from the doorway.
"Your leprosy puts all of us in a difficult position."

*Not as difficult as mine,* Nathaniel wanted to say but held his
tongue, reminding himself again that this couldn't be easy on
Edward. It had been nearly eight years, after all. Three years while
Nathaniel served the military in India, then five years since his
return. And now to discover his brother had leprosy. Were it
reversed, Nathaniel thought, he might be just as reserved toward
Edward as Edward now was toward him.

"Naturally, we will continue to feed you, as we will the baby," Edward continued. "Until we receive a reply to the letter already dispatched to the archbishop. We will let him guide us."

"Anything but a foundling hospital for the baby," Nathaniel said with passion.

"Ah yes, the letter pinned to her shawl. I found it this morning when I went to burn her clothes. Almost missed it. But I certainly read it. If I remember correctly, there was a great deal in there about not sending her to a foundling hospital."

"Especially in this parish," Nathaniel said with vehemence. "It's common knowledge that little of the taxes reaches the foundlings."

"I find it curious that you should care so much."

"Of course I care!" Edward's comment made no sense to Nathaniel. "You know as well as I do that they put children out as apprentices almost as soon as they can walk."

"That is somewhat of an exaggeration. Foundling hospitals have their purpose."

"Anything but a foundling hospital. That was the whole point of bringing her here!"

"Again, I find it curious that you seem to care so deeply for this baby's welfare. And I refuse to speculate at the archbishop's decision. Our natural fear is that the baby, too, has leprosy. If so, that will make it much more difficult to decide her fate."

"The baby? She has a name. Gabrielle. Call her that. I can understand the need to treat me like a leper, but not Gabrielle."

"How can you be sure? We found her in your arms. Which, I might add, was a senseless way to put her at risk of contracting your disease. Now she must be held in quarantine."

"Quarantine?"

"Until we are certain she shows no symptoms."

"That's three years!" Nathaniel knew all too well what the medical world knew of leprosy.

"Three years? Oh dear."

"Can't you imagine how horrible that would be for her?"

"I am not the one who brought her here," Edward said stiffly, still trying to comprehend the length of quarantine. Surely the archbishop wouldn't make Gabrielle the commune's responsibility that long! Raising a child would most definitely interfere with the women's devotion to worship.

"It is highly unlikely she has the disease."

"Are you a physician?"

"No. Merely well read on this subject. Just last month one of the world's foremost experts on the subject published an article in a medical journal to proclaim that the fear of contagion is highly overrated. Why, Dr. Cuplinn goes on to—"

"One expert? To the rest of the world, the mere act of holding her is enough to put her in danger. And through her, others. What if you had fled from here unnoticed? All of us here would have had contact with her. What if we had let her among other children? And what if they, like us here, had contracted leprosy because of her contact with you?"

Nathaniel nearly sighed. His brother's self-righteousness had not lessened at all over time. "At the very least, don't leave her in darkness to wither like a flower cut off from the sun."

"She must be quarantined. Because you held her in your arms, you gave us no choice. What would possess you to risk her health, even if, as you claim, the disease has little likelihood of spreading?"

"She would have died otherwise."

Edward waved the letter in his hand. "Are you saying my brother threatened to kill her unless you agreed to bring her here?"

"Your . . . your brother." Nathaniel's strained voice dropped almost to silence. Did Edward not know that he faced his brother at this moment?

"My brother." Edward waved the letter again. "The man responsible for this note. And, I assume, responsible for the baby. I have no doubt he left the mother as well. It's not the first family he's done this to."

Now Edward's questions about Nathaniel's concern for the baby made sense. Edward believed him to be a messenger, someone hired by Nathaniel to deliver the baby.

And why not, decided Nathaniel after stunned reflection. Leprosy had distorted his face. His vocal cords were raspy. He wore a hooded cloak to keep himself hidden, even now.

Edward continued to wave the letter and spoke a touch impatiently. "I want to know the circumstances that led you to take a baby and this letter from my brother. Do you know the man? Where is he now? He abandoned his wife. At the very least I would like to make him face her. He sent her a letter too. Can you imagine that? Too cowardly to tell her in person. Let me repeat, tell me now if you know his whereabouts."

*Let me repeat, tell me now if you know his whereabouts.*

Nathaniel almost blurted out the truth. In this moment, once again, he faced the same agonizing decision that had confronted him on the ship returning from India. When he recognized the first symptoms of leprosy. He loved his Suzanne and Ethan and Faith far too much to want to expose them to his disease. Even had he known of Dr. Cuplinn's opinion years earlier, he then shared the prejudice against leprosy and feared the contagion. Nor could Nathaniel bear the thought of forcing his family to watch him slowly rot away. He did not want to make them have to choose to remove themselves from society and stay with him. Most of all, he feared they might choose the opposite, to cast him away forever. He couldn't send Suzanne a letter that he had died; it would have been too difficult to successfully fabricate the circumstances of his death. So he'd anguished over the letter that she finally did receive before Christmas, the one that told her he loved another woman.

"The man who gave this to you," Edward repeated. "Tell me about him. Did he know you were a leper when he approached you? Where did you meet him?"

And now, if Nathaniel reached out to his brother, would his brother reach back with open arms? Or shudder once again in horror? If his beloved Suzanne finally discovered the truth, would she want to see him? How could he inflict his hideous face upon Ethan and Faith?

Earlier, when Nathaniel believed the decision had been taken out of his hands, he was relieved. Now, again, it was his choice. Declare himself. Or stay hidden.

"Will you not speak?" Edward demanded. "The man who gave you this letter is a rogue. Hide him not. He deserves no mercy."

*He deserves no mercy.*

Nathaniel bowed his head. "Where I lived, the people believed me to be badly burned. I only ventured out late at night while the city slept. Roaming the streets near the docks. With my face and hands hidden should I happen upon any stranger."

"It was there you met him. On the streets? He threatened to kill the baby if you did not help?"

"Threatened to kill the baby?"

"You told me that the baby would have died without your help."

"That is true. Without my help, she would have been abandoned. As for your brother, I have nothing to tell you."

"Nothing?" Edward said.

"Nothing," Nathaniel replied. "Please, leave me in peace."

So the door shut upon him, leaving Nathaniel in darkness, with only tiny shafts of pure light between mortar cracks to remind him that the sun shone outside his prison.

.

IMA UNCEREMONIOUSLY SWUNG the door open to the attic
room that held Gabrielle.

Gabrielle was sitting in the center, entertaining herself by
chewing on the toes of her left foot.

"Bah?" Gabrielle said, happy to have company. Grinning with
delight, she dropped her foot and crawled as fast as she could
toward her visitor.

"Haven't you any other words?" Gabrielle's smile irked Ima.
*Let other people get sentimental over babies.* And Ima could not be
charmed, because all her life, anyone who had tried to charm her was
overlooking her inherent ugliness to try to get something from her.

"Bah," Gabrielle answered.

"Bah, yourself," Ima warned from behind her linen mask. "I'm

47

here with more porridge. And if you spill this one, there will be no more. Understand?"

Ima stepped inside, swinging the door shut behind her by balancing on one foot and hitting it with the heel of her other foot. She couldn't use her hands. In her left was a bowl of porridge, spoon resting inside. Her other hand was draped with clothes for the baby's bottom.

She set the bowl down.

"Bah!" Gabrielle darted toward it.

With her hands wrapped in linen cloth, Ima could allow contact with the baby. She leaned down and pushed her away from the bowl. "Not until you're clean."

"Bah?"

"Clean, I said. We can't have you smelling like a gutter rat, even if that's where you've spent your life. After all—" Ima stopped. "There is no reason to talk to this child," she admonished herself. "It's ridiculous. She can't understand a thing."

"Bah? Bah?"

"Humph." Ima squatted and rolled Gabrielle onto her belly to remove her clothing. This was horrible work, but Ima was not going to allow Reverend Terwillegar to think she would be defeated by a baby.

Gabrielle squirmed hard, protesting this unfamiliar position. Ima pushed her down.

Gabrielle expressed her dissatisfaction with a howl.

"All right then," Ima said. "We'll try it this way." Still squatting, she rolled Gabrielle over.

"Bah!" Gabrielle said, happy to see Ima's face again.

"Humph." Ima had always had clumsy fingers. The linen

48

wrapped around them made her task even more difficult. But Gabrielle had patience and continued to smile as Ima peeled back her clothing.

When she finally discovered the source of the smell, Ima wrinkled her nose at the contents of the cloth wrapped around Gabrielle's bottom. *Green! Is this normal? What had the baby been eating?*

"Bah!" Gabrielle said.

Despite her queasiness, Ima couldn't help but smile beneath her mask. *"Bah* is certainly correct. Perhaps I should get a cork for you."

"Bah."

Ima reached for her clothes and pins. As she did, Gabrielle grinned and with a quick right hand, reached down to the messy contents beneath her bottom.

"Bah!" Gabrielle held up her dirty hand in triumph and squeezed the contents between her fingers. Such an interesting sensation.

"Aaaawk!" Ima exclaimed. "No! Bad baby! No!"

Ima grabbed Gabrielle's hand, groaning as her pure white linens immediately became stained green. Gabrielle grinned and used her other free hand to reach down.

"No! Bad baby! No!"

Too late.

Discreet coughing from the doorway. Because Ima had not closed the door completely, Reverend Terwillegar had been able to silently push it open again.

How much had he seen? Ima wondered, with instant anger at her vulnerability.

"Need assistance?" Reverend Terwillegar did a poor job of hiding a smirk. Ima had the poor thing pinned down, and from his perspective, looked all the more ridiculous because her face and hands were covered with the white strips of linen. "I've changed a few babies in my time. Sisters and all, you know."

"Certainly not!" Ima said. She did not like the implication that she was not woman enough to handle this simple task. "Now remove yourself. This is an uncovered female!"

"As you wish." Reverend Terwillegar sauntered away. His cheerful whistling reached her from down the hallway.

Five minutes later, Ima had it all cleaned up. She'd been forced to remove most of the once-white linen from her hands, and now only two precious strips protected her from possible contamination by contact.

Ima propped Gabrielle against the wall, then turned to get her porridge.

Gabrielle immediately scooted forward and tried to clutch at Ima's legs. "Bah! Bah!" Gabrielle grinned.

Ima sighed. She set Gabrielle back against the wall. She dropped to her knees and tried to shove a spoonful of porridge at Gabrielle's face before the baby moved again.

With no success.

Gabrielle tried to crawl up Ima's thighs. "Bah?"

"For heaven's sake," Ima said. "You are a vexing child."

"Bah." Gabrielle liked hearing Ima's voice.

"Very well, then." With her free arm, Ima scooped Gabrielle up and held her to her chest. Ima turned awkwardly so she could lean against the wall. From that position, she used her other hand to dip the spoon into the porridge bowl, then lift it to Gabrielle's mouth.

"Are you finally satisfied, you little urchin?" Ima asked with a smile, completely forgetting that she'd decided it was useless to talk to a baby who couldn't understand words.

Gabrielle swallowed the porridge and came up for air. "Bah," she announced her happiness again. "Bah."

"Hush," Ima said, still unaware that she was smiling behind her linen mask. She fed another spoonful to Gabrielle. "Just eat so that I can be gone."

Ima smiled again and gave Gabrielle more porridge.

"Tell me," Nathaniel said to his brother an hour later. His bandaged ankle was straight out in front of him. He had positioned straw between his back and the wall as a pillow to lean against. "This ne'er-do-well brother of yours. The one who abandoned his wife . . ."

Reverend Terwillegar had intended to push a plate of potatoes and ham through the open doorway, then quickly leave. But the voice of the leper stopped him as he was shutting the door.

"What about him?" Reverend Terwillegar's tone was sharp. He did not like being reminded of his brother and the horrible pall that hung over their family's reputation because of Nathaniel.

"Actually, I'm more curious about his wife. Surely she must have done something to deserve his treatment."

"Nothing could be further from the truth! She was devoted to him."

"Unattractive perhaps?"

"How impudent! To insult a woman you've never seen. Especially one of such fairness."

"So she remarried immediately, I suppose. After all, one that fair must have had no end of suitors."

"On the contrary." Reverend Terwillegar wanted to leave

immediately. Who knew how the foul air from inside the shed might send something creeping into his lungs. "The men lined up to court her, but she pined for my brother grievously. Such was her love. She told me repeatedly that it would have been far better if he died. Then, at least, she would not cling to the hope that he might reappear someday. Or that she would stop looking for him around each corner every time she went forth into the city."

Nathaniel's eyes stung with tears. He was glad for the darkness of the shed. "She is alone now, then?"

"What business is this of yours?" Reverend Terwillegar answered.

"None," Nathaniel lied. "None at all. But the hours are long here, and I think often about the man who sent me with the baby. So, too, do I wonder about the woman he abandoned. She . . . she has not married at all in the years that passed."

"She is now betrothed."

"Ah. To a good man, I would hope."

"To a very good man. She is about to be granted a divorce. They are to be wed on the Sabbath ahead."

*Suzanne is only days away from marriage.*

"Although . . . ," Edward continued.

"Yes?"

"You have a curious way of drawing me out," Reverend Terwillegar said. His words came out in short bursts, because he breathed through his mouth to avoid the odor from within the shed. "But if you have part of the story, you should know more of it. She visits me occasionally and pours her heart out to me. I am, after all, a man of the cloth. And . . ."

"Yes?"

"Even now, days away from marriage, she is unsure. She tells me . . ."

"Yes?"

"She wonders if it is fair to marry a man for convenience. She does not love him. She wants her children to have a father. But . . ."

"Yes?"

"I only speak her confidences because you do not know her. She cannot even bear the thought of his arms around her or his lips touching hers. After all these years, she still loves the man who abandoned her for another woman. My brother—" Reverend Terwillegar's voice rose in anger—"does not deserve that kind of love."

"I see," Nathaniel said. It was on his lips to utter who he was. If his beloved Suzanne still cared for him, perhaps she would not be repulsed by his appearance.

*No!* Nathaniel told himself sharply. No human would ever look on him with anything but horror.

"Is that all of your questions?" Reverend Terwillegar said, hand on the edge of the half-shut door. "Nothing further to say."

"Nothing further."

The door closed.

Leaving Nathaniel with his memories of the woman he loved just as fiercely as she loved him.

8

AS IMA TRIED TO FALL ASLEEP, she could not get the last image of Gabrielle out of her head. That of Gabrielle's face turned upward in trust, watching Ima's eyes as the door shut in the final light of day.

Gabrielle was alone. In the dark. In a small attic.

Ima could not bear it.

With an exasperated sigh, she lit a lamp. She dressed. She went through the laborious process of wrapping her face and hands in new linen strips. She walked to the door and opened it and peeked down the hallway to make sure no one would see her. She stepped outside her room, hesitated, then returned inside.

On the chest of drawers, legs splayed to keep it upright, was the only object she had kept from childhood. The doll her father had given her that night in drunken affection.

Ima took the doll and hurried to Gabrielle.

IN TOTAL DARKNESS, Nathaniel wept.

Before, at least he'd had a freedom of sorts.

Now?

Imprisoned by the shed, imprisoned by his body, imprisoned by his memories of his family, imprisoned by the anguish he felt for Gabrielle, Nathaniel had lost everything. He didn't even have the control or ability to end his own life.

From the depths of his suicidal depression, he uttered a short, desperate prayer: "Oh, Jesus, help me."

*Our Father which art in heaven, hallowed be Thy name. . . .*

Edward knelt at the foot of his bed, satisfied that his creaking knees provided enough pain for the humility required to approach God.

*Thy kingdom come. Thy will be done in earth, as it is in heaven. . . .*

As Edward spoke out loud, his mind drifted toward the tasks ahead of him the next day. As the only man in the commune, he was expected to handle the preaching and lead the prayers. Much as he would be relieved to see Miss Hogg take over some of the duties, he also knew he dare not give her even the slightest reason to demand more authority.

*Give us this day our daily bread. And forgive us our debts, as we forgive our debtors. . . .*

Not even God, he decided, would forgive his brother, Nathaniel, for what he'd done. Unless Nathaniel begged forgiveness, and how likely was that from someone who would abandon his family, then send a baby to the commune.

*And lead us not into temptation, but deliver us from evil. . . .*

If Gabrielle was Nathaniel's illegitimate offspring, did Edward truly have an obiligation?

*No!* he told himself. And this was certainly something he would keep secret from Miss Hogg. The safest way to deliver himself from the evil one was to give her no excuse to harangue him in any way.

"Amen," Edward announced to finish his prayer.

He stood, grimacing with satisfaction that his knees hurt so badly.

The best approach was a penitent approach. Perhaps he would base his next sermon on that very subject.

IMA HAD INTENDED simply to leave the doll with Gabrielle.

Instead, she found it too comforting to hold the little baby.

As the lamp oil slowly burned to empty, Ima sang half-remembered lullabies to Gabrielle.

Each fell asleep, holding the other.

THERE HAD BEEN A SUNDAY, only three months before the night he brought Gabrielle to the commune, that Nathaniel had seen what he needed to see at the church. Suzanne had arrived with a man who guided her arms and helped the children in and out of the church.

Her fiancé.

NATHANIEL HAD CONFIRMED that through an inquiry to the barrister who had handled the monthly payments to Suzanne since the retirement of William Morgan.

A fiancé.

Another man would take his place. At Nathaniel's dinner table. With his children. And with his wife.

Much as these thoughts were like a knife in his heart, Nathaniel also knew that another man could now provide for the woman and children he loved. Much better than Nathaniel had with his small monthly pension. Another man would protect the woman and children he loved. Much better than Nathaniel was able to by watching over the cottage each night.

The burden had been lifted from Nathaniel. He need not worry about their well-being.

With that lifted burden, Nathaniel had also lost his only purpose. He was free to do what he had wished to do for so long.

End his life.

So three months before, Nathaniel had stood at the edge of the docks, in the darkness two hours before dawn. The drop was less than ten feet, and the water was deep enough to hold the massive ships that hid him from any passersby.

He had wrapped heavy chains around his feet. These were not to hold him down long enough to drown. He could not swim, so the chains were not necessary to kill him. Instead, he wished for his body to sink far beneath the oily water into thick sediment to cloak the final ravages of his death from the eyes of the living.

The dirty water of the Thames slapped at the hulls of the moored ships. A mad howl reached him from somewhere in the depths of the slums behind him, rising and rising in an eerily beautiful crescendo until softly dying in the night.

He wondered if he should pray.

He knew, however, it would be a hollow prayer. He refused to believe in a God who would take his family from him in the manner that it occurred.

Nathaniel felt nothing. Not even relief. Soon, all his sadness would be taken from him.

He shuffled forward, with the chains clanking slightly around his legs.

He prepared to topple forward, forcing the thought of the brief agony ahead out of his mind.

Then . . .

Nathaniel had heard quiet mewling from a mound of fishnet piled carelessly near one of the smaller ships moored by heavy rope. Mewling, as if a cat had been drawn by the scent of dead fish to become entangled in the netting.

The noise distracted Nathaniel from his task. He listened again, for there was a strangeness to the mewling. The mewling had an oddly human echo to it.

As quickly as he could, Nathaniel hobbled forward to the fishnet. With hands feeling nothing, Nathaniel took care not to pull too hard as he lifted the narrow coarse roping. Even though he intended to end his life, he could not escape the routines that had preserved his body against much of the damage of leprosy.

The ship's masts and webbing cast a corrugated shadow on Nathaniel as he lifted layer after layer of net. To anyone at a distance, Nathaniel's hooded outline might have appeared like that of a witch pulling at herbs rooted deep in the ground.

As he set aside each layer, the mewling did not diminish.

Finally, Nathaniel reached the source of the mewling.

And stopped in disbelief. Then amazement, unsure that he understood correctly what he had found.

He shifted slightly to let moonlight pour on the remainder of netting. From the shadows, a tiny hand reached up for him. Without thinking, Nathaniel reached down. Trusting fingers closed around his thumb. The mewling ceased.

"Dear God," Nathaniel whispered, "a foundling in rags."

He pried the baby's fingers loose from his thumb. Nathaniel was no expert on babies, but he guessed this one to be less than a year old. Girl, if the hair was a clue to its sex. But it was a child of the slums . . .

Here, mothers abandoned by husbands were as common as rats and much less prosperous. As were babies left to the care of the parish by these harried, impoverished mothers—babies doomed to be apprenticed in the rough trades or sent to the factories as early as four years of age.

Just a slum child.

It tried to sit in a vain effort to reach Nathaniel, then fell because of the unstable foundation of the remaining pile of netting.

The baby gurgled. Moonlight showed that it was smiling.

"See if you'll still have me after this," Nathaniel said.

He pulled back his hood and squatted close, turning to let the moonlight play across his face and chest. He tightened his jaw in anticipation of the child's reaction. *It is old enough,* he guessed, *to know horror.*

The baby's eyes met his, and once again the tiny hand reached upward. Nathaniel let its fingers grasp his thumb again.

"Ba-ba-ba?"

Nathaniel could not resist the temptation.

"Only for a moment." Nathaniel lifted the child from the netting. He held it to his chest. The baby clutched his neck and sighed contentment.

Tears had blurred Nathaniel's vision that night.

Before this, the last time he had had physical contact with another human was that day just before Christmas, years earlier, when the solicitor William Morgan had reached out to shake his hand good-bye.

# 10

IN AN ELABORATE FORMAL GARDEN near Westminster
Abbey, a tall man stared at two white swans on a quiet pond. He
looked behind him at the approach of a second, whose footsteps
were easily heard on the cobblestone walk.

This man was short and broad, with unruly red hair. The material of his suit jacket, although appropriately dark for an appointment with the archbishop's assistant, was coarse and well worn.
This man, however, had worn the appropriate color entirely by
accident; it was his only jacket. Nor would he have cared had he
known that the untidiness of his clothing and appearance offended
the other man, which it did.

"I trust you have found another poor soul that you want to
ship away?" The redheaded man ran his fingers through his hair as

he asked his question. Not to make the hair neater, but to push locks out of his vision. He hadn't cut his hair in months.

"I believe, Dr. Cuplinn, that I suggested this appointment fully one hour earlier," the tall man said. He was tall by any standard and seemed much taller beside the short Dr. Cuplinn. This man's dark hair was slicked back, and his walrus mustache glistened with the same oil. His vest and suit matched perfectly and fit him the way custom-tailored clothing should. "You have kept me waiting."

"Palliser, you're far down the line when it comes to my time." Dr. Cuplinn had a thick Scottish brogue. "The woman with a breeched birth mattered far more to me than the offer of tea and crumpets with you. If you want to see me according to your schedule, perhaps you'll travel to the East End and meet me there."

Dr. Palliser made sure he kept his distance from Dr. Cuplinn and hid a flinch of distaste. First, it bothered him that Dr. Cuplinn refused to return the courtesy of addressing him by title. It was true that Nigel Palliser had not practiced medicine in years, but he still deserved to be called doctor. Second, the thought of mingling with smells and sweatiness and disease of the common folk of the East End was enough to compel him to send a servant to run a hot bath. And third? Well, the man dealt with lepers. Infrequently, to be sure, but one could never assume it was safe to be near another who spent time with lepers.

"I represent the archbishop," Dr. Palliser replied. "It hardly suits the dignity of his office for me to go running in all directions."

Dr. Cuplinn snorted. "You represent yourself. Now get on with it. You only send for me when another leper has appeared. Will this one be shipped in a sumptuous cabin or belowdecks like a slave?"

"I hardly think that your presumptions are necessary."

"Why is it, then," Dr. Cuplinn asked, "that the rich are sent to a foreign private hospital in total secrecy at great expense to them, and yet you have me ship the poor ones abroad in miserable quarantined quarters belowdecks?"

"Economics is an unavoidable fact of life. And God blesses those he favors."

"So the poor deserve their lot?"

"In a manner of speaking, yes. And I've noticed you never refuse the fees we pay you to assist the wealthy."

"Because that money allows me to help the less fortunate," Dr. Cuplinn answered. He spread his arms to indicate the peace and beauty of their surroundings. "Revolutionary concept, wouldn't you agree? Heaven forbid this garden lose any luster by diverting money from here to, say, a starving child."

"I have no need for your commentary."

"Have you brought my request to the archbishop?" Dr. Cuplinn asked.

"That the church fund a place where lepers can live here in England?"

"The same request I deliver each time we meet."

"He is considering it," Dr. Palliser said.

"And you lie to me."

"You are an obnoxious man."

"Finally, you speak truthfully. Now give me the name and address of the unfortunate, and I'll make my inspection and report accordingly."

Dr. Palliser didn't reply but reached inside his jacket. He pulled out a folded letter and handed it to Dr. Cuplinn. "We received this letter yesterday. I believe it will tell you everything you need to know."

Dr. Cuplinn scanned it. "A man and a baby." He handed the letter back. "It seems to me that the quarantine issue has been taken care of. And your secrecy issue. The church knows how to protect its own."

Dr. Palliser ignored the jibe. "By the description provided, it is easy to guess the man has obviously been unreported for years. If he just came off a ship, we need to know which one would allow a leper in that condition on board. If he arrived with it undetected years earlier, then he has been roaming London ever since. We need to know where he has been and who has been in contact with him."

"That is your problem. Mine is assisting him in whatever way I can."

Dr. Palliser sighed. "Yes, that is our problem. The archbishop has already sent back a letter requesting that the Reverend Terwillegar inquire into the man's background. But if in any of your conversations with this leper you can find out his history . . ."

"What is spoken to me in confidence stays in confidence."

"Even the merest hint would suffice."

"What is spoken to me in confidence stays in confidence. That, along with my expertise in this area, is precisely why you retain me again and again."

"It certainly isn't your manners."

Dr. Cuplinn flashed a rare smile. "Such forthrightness. Twice now in one conversation. I encourage you to make that a habit."

Dr. Palliser chose to ignore that remark. "You'll take care of this then?"

"First thing tomorrow. Send a carriage and driver."

"As you wish." Dr. Palliser gave a mocking bow. But it was wasted.

. Cuplinn had already spun on his heels to walk away.

*Amazing grace! how sweet the sound—that saved a wretch like me! . . .*

Women's voices filled the morning quiet in sweet harmony, ringing off the stone walls that surrounded Reverend Terwillegar.

*I once was lost but now am found, was blind but now I see.*

Centuries earlier, the grounds of the estate had been designed around an ancient stone church, for the first lord to inherit the land from Henry XIII had been a religious man and wanted his serfs to be able to worship. While the church had fallen into disrepair, it had never been torn down.

For Miss Hogg, the existence of the church building had been a wonderful opportunity. As part of her proposal to the archbishop, Miss Hogg had promised to rebuild the interior of the church, and so it was that after hundreds of years of neglect, once again it held worshipers.

*'Twas grace that taught my heart to fear, and grace my fears relieved; how precious did that grace appear the hour I first believed!*

There were twenty women, and the ancient church was so small that the hardwood pews seemed entirely full. Sun beamed on them through delicately designed stained-glass windows. Reverend Terwillegar beamed on them from his pulpit at the front.

His congregation consisted of women of differing ages, each in a dark gray dress, each with hair pinned back, each with eyes on the cross above the pulpit as they sang their usual morning worship songs.

The reverend's smiling face, however, hid his concern. A leper held prisoner. A baby shut in darkness. And all of it waited on word from the archbishop.

*The Lord has promised good to me, his word my hope secures;*
*he will my shield and portion be as long as life endures.*

And now, Reverend Terwillegar thought, the archbishop's first reply was not a decision but a request. One that would force Reverend Terwillegar to spend yet more time with the leper. Not even the wonderful words and music of this hymn brought joy.

In the meantime, there was the need to keep a stiff upper lip and pretend all was well.

Reverend Terwillegar continued to beam down at the women as they sweetly sang in unison. As a group, their singing had improved greatly over the last months, and now—in normal circumstances—it was an actual joy to worship with them.

*Through many dangers, toils and snares I have already come; 'tis*
*grace hath brought me safe thus far, and grace will lead me home.*

The harmony of their collective voices carried outside the church and across the estate grounds.

Their sweet voices reached Nathaniel, stuck in the straw in the corner of his makeshift prison. His leg had begun to swell, and he felt warmth on the inside of his thigh. It was a sensation he welcomed, for so little of his body provided him any sensation.

*When we've been there ten thousand years, bright shining as the sun, we've no less days to sing God's praise than when we'd first begun.*

Unlike his brother, Nathaniel listened with some gratitude.

*Amazing grace! how sweet the sound—that saved a wretch like me! I once was lost but now am found, was blind but now I see.*

And Nathaniel listened with some degree of sorrow.

He had long given up hope that he would be able to be part of anything that joined people together.

"BAH?"

Beneath her linen mask, Ima smiled at Gabrielle's greeting. This time, she had opened the door to see Gabrielle vainly trying to catch flies on the wall.

"Come here, little urchin."

Ima moved toward Gabrielle with confidence. She changed Gabrielle's soiled clothes quickly and scooped her up to hold her and feed her spooned porridge.

Gabrielle's eyes widened slightly at the first mouthful, and Ima was watching for it.

"Extra sugar and extra cream," Ima informed Gabrielle. "Makes a difference, doesn't it?"

Gabrielle answered by opening her mouth wide and holding it open to wait for the next spoonful.

Again, Ima smiled beneath her mask. She sat against the wall, with Gabrielle wrapped to her body with her left arm. Ima used her right hand to dip the spoon in the bowl of porridge on the floor.

As Ima continued to feed, Gabrielle reached down at the arm that held her. Gabrielle plucked at the new white linens wrapped around Ima's left hand. Gabrielle managed to pull one end loose. She tugged hard.

"Bah," Gabrielle announced between swallows of the delight-ful-tasting porridge.

"Bah, bah," Ima said. "Leave that alone." But Ima didn't stop Gabrielle from playing with the loose end.

Ima held Gabrielle for several minutes after feeding her, with Gabrielle running her fingers across the linen mask. Gabrielle stared unblink-ing into Ima's eyes, the only part of Ima's face that was exposed.

"Mah?" Gabrielle had been experimenting with new conso-nants, and this seemed as good a time as any to try it again. "Mah?"

To Ima, it sounded like "ma-ma." An unfamiliar emotion over-whelmed her, a flooding of tenderness and joy.

"Mah?"

"Bah," Ima said, fighting this sensation of weakness. "Bah."

"Mah," Gabrielle said, satisfied with the new sound. "Mah."

"No," Ima said suddenly and sternly. She feared this new emotion and set Gabrielle down and stood. "I'm not your mama."

72

Gabrielle reached for and clung to Ima's dress. The loose end of linen dangled down tantalizingly within Gabrielle's grasp. Naturally, she grabbed. Then lost her balance.

Still in the clutch of Gabrielle's hand, the strip of linen unfurled downward, nearly unraveling completely.

"Bah," Ima said. She quickly began to rewrap her hand. Focused on this task, she didn't notice as Gabrielle scooted toward the open door. When Ima finished the hasty rewrap, she looked around.

Gabrielle had disappeared.

Her delighted giggles came from outside the room.

"Oh, my heavens!" Ima said. She found Gabrielle outside at the top of the stairs.

"No, no, no!" Ima told Gabrielle. "I don't want to see you hurt!"

"Mah?"

"Yes, ma-ma." Ima scooped her upward and held her tight.

"Mah," Gabrielle answered firmly. "Mah."

"I don't want to see you hurt," Ima repeated. "Not ever."

# 11

"I HAVE HEARD from the archbishop." Edward's voice was muffled behind the perfumed handkerchief pressed against his mouth and nose. "He wished for me to inquire as to how and when you contracted leprosy, how long you have been in London with it, and as to where you stayed."

Nathaniel welcomed the fresh air and glimpse of flowers and grass beyond where Edward stood in the doorway again.

"What has he decided about Gabrielle?" Nathaniel rustled in the straw, easing his sore back. Since he couldn't stand, he stretched as often as possible.

"No decision. He wants information first."

"If he is that concerned about me, why not visit himself?"

"I believe he is far more concerned about the Church of

England. Miss Hogg said it herself. If the Church of England can be seen heading off an epidemic by nipping it in the bud, so much the better."

"Epidemic."

"There have been no lepers, really, since the Middle Ages. How horrifying if suddenly—"

"If suddenly I was the cause of streets filled with them?"

"Yes, that sums it rather precisely."

*I am your brother,* Nathaniel wanted to say. *I am not an object. Treat me as if I am human, as if I have feelings.*

Instead, Nathaniel forced himself to be detached. Truth be told, he hardly felt human himself. Were it not for the time he'd spent with Gabrielle, surely he would have gone insane from his self-imposed isolation.

"How much do you know about leprosy?" Nathaniel asked calmly.

"What everyone knows. Contagious. Rots off body parts and such." Finally, Edward realized what he sounded like. "You'll pardon me for saying so."

"I've already informed you it's not as contagious as you think. I've made it a point to read as much as possible. Nor does it rot off the body parts. What it does is take away all sensation. So if one doesn't take care, a blister turns into an infected ulcer. And that ulcer into flesh that wears away. And so on. My ankle, for example, gives me no pain. During my days in London, I ended and began every day by carefully examining my hands and my feet for any cuts or scrapes, knowing if I did not tend to it immediately, the condition would worsen to my detriment. Leprosy does not kill. I am five years into it and could survive another twenty, if I took proper care of my body."

Nathaniel held out his hands, extending them past his cloak. His fingers had begun to curl as the tendons slowly but inevitably shrunk. "I cannot feel the softness of Gabrielle's skin. I cannot smell her hair. I can't even taste food. That is the life of a leper."

"Quite," Edward said, pressing the handkerchief harder against his face. "Indeed." He coughed, anxious to end this line of conversation. "If you would be kind enough to answer the archbishop's questions . . ."

"First, tell me about your brother," Nathaniel said. "What was his name? Nathaniel?"

"I've told you the salient points. Upon his return from India, he informed his wife that he had fallen in love with another woman, and he abandoned his family. Obviously, he has done it once again, this time involving you."

"I see. He left his wife penniless?"

"No, he provided her with a monthly income that barely takes care of her needs."

"He didn't abandon her completely, then. No one sees this?"

"Why do you care?" Edward asked. "For once again you have returned to the subject of my brother."

"Just curious. It strikes me as odd that someone seen as such a heartless cad would take care of his family in such a way."

"Probably just a price he is willing to pay to appease his conscience as he chases other skirts."

"A shame."

"I agree. It's scandalous."

"No," Nathaniel said. "A shame you would make that assumption."

"What other assumption could one make? The facts are there."

"What was he like before he went to India?" Nathaniel asked. "Where did you grow up? Did you get along together as brothers?"

"I'm the oldest. Accordingly, I'm to inherit the estate. He fell madly in love and went into the military as a way to build his career. You know, connections and that sort. He would have done well too. He was dashing, brave. Cut a very romantic figure. Blessed with tremendous athleticism. Had it all, except for the inheritance. But we had no doubt he would make his way in the world just fine. I expected that in the end, he would be worth far more financially than I, even after my inheritance. Although he didn't know it, I was always quite envious of him. That was, of course, until he behaved so miserably after his return. Leaving his wife and children, never to be heard from again. No one thinks of him any longer as dashing, brave, or romantic."

"I guess not," Nathaniel said, finding irony in the truth of that. Who would find a leper dashing, brave, or romantic?

"Strange," Edward mused. "As he and I grew up together, I always felt vaguely inferior. And now, as it turns out, I was a much superior person. I, at least, have lived up to responsibilities. He has condemned himself by his actions. And I belong to the church."

"I see," Nathaniel said.

"Is that enough? Will you give me what I need for the archbishop?"

"How and when I contracted leprosy? Where I stayed in London? As to the first, that is not his business. And tell him there are no others. I made sure of that. I've kept myself in isolation, except to roam the streets in the late hours of night."

"How? Surely you must have eaten."

"I stayed in a room above a pub. My meals were served, at my

78

request, by placing them in front of the door. I blunted curiosity by telling them I had been horribly burned in a fire. And that was it."

Again, Edward coughed. "Not quite."

"Not quite?"

"The archbishop insisted on finding out the address of your abode. The public health department will paint it with white lime. No one else need be infect—" Edward stopped himself—"affected by your condition."

"White lime."

"It has been effective during the cholera epidemics."

"Of course." Nathaniel thought of the final letter he had left behind, the diaries he wanted his wife to find. The pub owner would go inside at the end of the month to seek rent and discover the package to be mailed. Now would not be the best time for Suzanne to discover it. "I'm not sure I want to tell you where I stayed. Rest assured, no one has access to it."

"That may not be good enough for the archbishop."

"It will have to be good enough."

"Remember, you are a prisoner. You depend on us for food."

"What I want," Nathaniel said, "is to sit outside. I have so few pleasures. Let me see the colors and hear the birds."

What Nathaniel wanted much more was to see Gabrielle. But he couldn't show too much concern. For it might lead Edward to more questions. Edward, after all, believed that Nathaniel was an anonymous beggar who had happened to accept money to deliver the baby on behalf of a man anxious to rid himself of a problem child.

"Where is your abode?"

"No," Nathaniel answered. If it was discovered where he had lived, too much else in there would be discovered. Letters, diaries.

"Good-bye then."

Again, Edward shut his brother into darkness.

"BAH?" This time it was Ima calling out the familiar greeting to Gabrielle.

"Mah!" Gabrielle stood against the far wall, with Ima's doll at her feet.

"Bah," Ima said, uncaring that much of her vocabulary had been reduced to one-syllable words. "Bah."

In her excitement, Gabrielle turned too quickly. She began to fall but instinctively placed her right foot forward. Momentum carried her, and to keep her balance, she moved her left foot ahead. Then her right.

With wobbly, lurching steps she walked toward the door.

Ima was mesmerized.

Gabrielle shouted with delight, and in her exuberance, tried to run to Ima. She fell hard and began to cry.

Ima rushed into the room and picked Gabrielle up and held her, swaying from side to side to comfort her tears. Gabrielle nestled her head into the crook of Ima's neck.

"You walked," Ima murmured into Gabrielle's ears. "I saw your first steps. I saw your first steps."

Gabrielle's cries lessened.

Ima had never held Gabrielle this close to her face before. The other times, she'd been careful to keep Gabrielle lower, against her belly and chest. Now, through her linen mask, Ima became aware for the first time of the smell of the little baby.

Ima stroked the back of Gabrielle's head.

Suddenly, it wasn't enough just to hold and smell Gabrielle. Ima craved to touch the softness of Gabrielle's fine hair and the skin of her neck.

Ima set Gabrielle down briefly. Gabrielle crawled back toward her and held her legs.

Ima unwrapped the slightest portion of her right hand, so that the fingertips were exposed. Surely, she told herself, there would be no harm in this. Especially if she washed her fingertips carefully afterward.

She lifted Gabrielle again and hugged her to her neck. Gabrielle wrapped her arms around Ima's neck.

Then Ima breathed in the baby smell again and lightly touched the back of Gabrielle's head, marveling at the sensation of the softness of hair and skin.

Was this what a mother felt with her own child?

Ima pondered this and did not fight against the overwhelming joy and tenderness that made it feel like she would burst.

Gabrielle sighed with contentment and fell asleep as Ima continued to gently stroke her.

# 12

"YOU MAY CEASE with this noise now." Reverend Terwillegar's shout interrupted Nathaniel's banging on the door with his tin water cup. Nathaniel stopped.

"What is the purpose of all this noise?" Reverend Terwillegar asked.

"I need to speak to someone." Nathaniel found it difficult to find the strength to speak loud enough. He had exhausted himself by getting to his feet and hopping to the door.

"Then speak."

"Please. Open the door."

"If that's what you wanted, you know I can't do that."

"Let me see you as I speak."

"Then step back. Well back."

Nathaniel groaned with the effort, and when he reached the far wall, he collapsed.

"Are you away from the door?"

Nathaniel tried to answer, but nausea mushroomed through his body.

"Are you away from the door?"

Knowing the only way the door would open was if he spoke, Nathaniel groaned out a reply to his brother.

The iron latch scraped across wood. Reverend Terwillegar cautiously opened the door, then satisfied himself that Nathaniel was indeed at the back wall.

Reverend Terwillegar gagged against the smell that hit him. He held a hand over his mouth and nose and stepped quickly away.

Beneath his hood, Nathaniel carefully lifted his head. Enough to see. Not enough for his face to be seen. He lifted an arm to shield his eyes from the brightness of the sun that pierced his prison through the now open door.

"I believe my ankle is terribly infected," Nathaniel said. "Please let me sit outside where I can examine it in the light."

"We will not risk anyone with exposure to leprosy."

"Leave the door open. I'll sit just inside."

"Where was your abode?" Edward's voice was muffled by his hand over his mouth. Even away from the shed, the smell of the leper was overpowering.

"If you won't let me help myself, then provide me something to end my life quickly."

"Sir, I must get back to my duties." Reverend Terwillegar shut the door again, closing out the sunshine and leaving Nathaniel in the dank straw.

# ❧ THE LEPER ❧

IT WAS SUCH A BOTHER to wrap her hands, and such a bother to try to change soiled clothes and to feed Gabrielle with fingers bound by linen, that Ima decided she would simply go in bare-handed and wash carefully later.

That, at least, was the excuse she told herself as she left her room with layers of linen around her nose and mouth. Surely, she'd remain safe from contamination then.

So it was that the next time she entered the room to be with Gabrielle, Ima was able to hold the baby with unfettered fingers. And again, she marveled at the baby's softness.

"Mah?" Gabrielle asked, as Ima cooed and cuddled.

Something broke inside Ima as Gabrielle stared upward with big trusting eyes.

"All right then," Ima said. "See if you still gaze with such adoration. With this ugly face, I've sent grown men running, for I'm nothing more than a Hogg."

She began to peel the mask of linen off her face. Gabrielle's eyes held their gaze on her. "Remember, I've given you ample warning."

Strip by strip, Ima removed the linen. When the last piece fell away, she half expected Gabrielle to cry in fear.

"Mah?" Gabrielle said. Her little hands reached up for Ima's mouth. "Mah."

Ima felt warmth on her face and realized she had begun to cry.

Squeezing Gabrielle, Ima uttered a simple quiet declaration for the first time in her life to anyone.

"I love you," she said to Gabrielle. "I love you so much."

85

THE FIRST OF THE FEVER took Nathaniel as midnight approached. He felt it rising up his body from his infected leg, like a river of lava.

He reached for water, but it was all gone. He croaked out for help, but his cry was swallowed by the darkness.

The fever burned his mind, and he saw himself holding his children. Not Gabrielle, whom he loved as fiercely as he loved his own son and daughter. He saw himself with Suzanne. At the church. Walking hand in hand with her, with his two children trailing behind. In the same way he'd seen the stranger walk with them, the stranger that she was betrothed to marry.

Such was the strength of this vision that he believed he was there. Not locked in the straw.

It was with a smile that he fell into restless sleep.

And when the rats came, he did not wake as they began to nibble at his fingers.

IMA RETURNED to Gabrielle that night when the rest of the women had gone to sleep. As she strode down the hallway, Ima wore her mask of linen, worried that if Reverend Terwillegar saw her approach the baby without it, he would ask too many questions.

But Ima could not bear to step inside the room wearing her mask. To her, it seemed like a betrayal of the new level of trust she had given to Gabrielle.

Ima stood outside the door and set the lantern down. She

unwrapped the strips of linen, then opened the door, carrying the lamp at waist level.

Gabrielle was curled on the floor, holding the doll.

"Mah?" Gabrielle left the doll behind in her hurry to crawl to Ima.

Ima's heart lurched with joy. She set the lamp down and knelt, allowing Gabrielle to reach up and grab around her neck.

"Mah," Gabrielle said.

"I love you," Ima said. "I love you. I love you. I love you." She smiled and let Gabrielle run little fingers over her unprotected face.

Without thinking—as if the prayer had arrived in her heart delivered by an angel—Ima closed her eyes and spoke softly. "Dear God, please look over this little one. Thank you for the gift of love you have given us. Thank you for sending your Son to give us hope beyond this life."

The rest of Ima's prayer continued without words, and she felt wrapped in a blanket of invisible warmth as she communed with God without any sense of the passage of time.

When she finished, slowly the sensation of warmth disappeared. She could have easily believed it had been her imagination, but she knew without a doubt that God had touched her.

So this was faith, she marveled. This was belief and understanding and full acceptance of God! He was love and she shared in his love, and because of it, she could give love. No, because of it, she was *compelled* to share this love with others.

She felt as if she had stepped out of a cocoon and that God's breath was enough to lift her beautiful new wings. She let this new peace and understanding fill her, unaware that this was the first time in her life there was no shame in her heart.

Ima pushed away her fears about what Reverend Terwillegar had said about a three-year quarantine. She pushed away her fears about the archbishop's decision. She did not know him well, but she knew his reputation as a godly man. He would not callously allow any baby to be locked up for that long.

And, as she had the night before, Ima fell asleep with Gabrielle in her arms.

# 13

~~~

THREE MONTHS EARLIER, in the days that immediately
followed his discovery of the abandoned baby beneath the fishnets,
Nathaniel had let his letters remain untouched on a shelf in his
room above the pub. The baby took his full attention and devotion.

At first he had not named her.

On the dock the night he discovered her, Nathaniel had
decided that if he did not take her back to his room, she would
likely die. He had weighed the near certainty of her death as a
result against the more unlikely risk of her contracting his leprosy
by brief continued contact with him. For it had been his intention
to deliver her in the darkness of the next night to a foundling
hospital. And later, to return to the Thames to end his own life in
its waters.

Except . . .

During the first full day with her—as he waited for night to provide the cloak of darkness that would allow him to safely travel the streets to the foundling hospital—the baby girl captivated Nathaniel with her happy alertness.

That day strange sounds had burst from Nathaniel's mouth. Laughter. He had not talked to anyone in so long that even his words to the baby seemed strange.

She had crawled toward him again and again with obvious delight, and she threw her arms around his neck with great enthusiasm.

And captured his heart.

On the second day, he had named her.

Gabrielle.

And on the third day, he knew he would devote whatever remained of his life to her.

THEN CAME A KNOCK on the door to the room above the pub.

Not the usual double knock. But a single knock.

"Yes?" Nathaniel called out as Gabrielle played at his feet.

"I have heard noises in there for the last several days." It was the owner of the pub. A man of roundness. Round bare skull. Round large belly. "And you have requested extra food. This is a moral establishment. I do not expect you to have guests in there without permission."

*Moral establishment.* Nathaniel knew this was a poor excuse. It simply meant the owner of the pub wanted extra money if the room was being used by a second person.

"Yes. I am—" Nathaniel hesitated, hoping the lie he had prepared would work—"helping my sister for a while. She needs me to look after her baby during an extended illness."

"Double the rent, then," the owner shouted through the closed door.

Nathaniel had no way of getting the extra money through employment. But he had made his decision. If Gabrielle was going to be infected with leprosy, it would have already occurred. So she already had leprosy. Or she did not. Either way, it would make no difference whether she was here or in a foundling hospital. The care that Nathaniel could give her here was far better than the neglect she would face there. Indeed, in such an institution, he knew, among all the other children of the slums, Gabrielle would face a far greater chance of contracting a fatal disease. More than half of the orphans there died before age five.

"Double the rent," Nathaniel agreed to the man he could not see outside his door. Somehow, by scavenging during the nights, he would find a way to pay.

Gabrielle had given him life again. Hope.

And love.

# 14

WHEN THE SHADOW fell across his desk, Reverend Terwillegar glanced up from working on his sermon to see a tall man who held a wrapped package the size of a box that might carry shoes.

"Dr. Palliser, what an unexpected pleasure!" Reverend Terwillegar hastily rose from his desk to greet his visitor. In so doing, he knocked over his ink bottle, spilling the black fluid over the final notes of his sermon.

He pulled his handkerchief from his vest and mopped at the ink futilely, then realized his important guest was still standing. Reverend Terwillegar left the mess on his desk and advanced to greet Dr. Palliser, but when he extended his hand, saw how much ink covered his fingers, and with much embarrassment, withdrew his hand again.

Dr. Palliser allowed a regal nod for the benefit of Reverend Terwillegar. He smoothed his walrus mustache with a quick twirl of his fingers and showed large white teeth with an insincere smile.

"Obviously this is early in the day," Dr. Palliser explained. "I would have sent notice of my visit, but the archbishop deemed this too important to wait."

"Too important?"

"Shall I sit?" Dr. Palliser asked, a not-so-gentle reprimand at the reverend's lack of manners.

"Yes, yes, please." With his right palm, Reverend Terwillegar smacked his head at his absentmindedness, leaving a big gob of ink above his eyebrows.

Dr. Palliser chose the biggest leather chair, guessing it was the one Reverend Terwillegar usually preferred. Dr. Palliser was a big believer in human politics and felt it served his purposes best to always assert his power, in large ways or small.

"I have had a physician follow me in a second carriage," Dr. Palliser began. "His name is Dr. Cuplinn. He is an expert in leprosy. Shortly, he will tend to the leper. If he is in sufficient health, I believe the archbishop might make arrangements to have him shipped to a leper colony. That will be best for the leper."

"I suppose you might be correct," Reverend Terwillegar said, thinking of how terrible the journey would be, locked somewhere in the hold of a ship, thinking of how terrible it would be living among other lepers in a foreign country. He fervently hoped in that moment that he himself had not contracted the disease.

"Of course I'm correct." Dr. Palliser said, frowning at the

spectacle of the ink across Reverend Terwillegar's forehead. "The expenses will come from the church coffers. Very inconvenient, this whole air of hiding a leper's condition and the worry that if word gets out the entire city would panic."

Dr. Palliser had more important matters to discuss and pressed on. "You can see that I have a package. It comes directly from the archbishop's office."

Although anyone could have assumed it came from the archbishop's office—since Dr. Palliser was the archbishop's secretary—Dr. Palliser preferred to mention the archbishop as frequently as possible in all conversations. It confirmed repeatedly that Dr. Palliser held a very high position.

"I see that."

Reverend Terwillegar looked more closely at the package now resting in Dr. Palliser's lap. It was a square box wrapped in oilskin and tied securely. Where the strings crossed, a medallion of wax showed the archbishop's seal.

"The archbishop believes you'll find it of great interest."

"What is in it?"

"I suppose you'll discover that when you open it." Dr. Palliser did not hide his irritation. What he did hide, however, was the reason for his irritation. The package had been sealed when the archbishop gave it to him, and the archbishop had declined to say what it held, ordering that Dr. Palliser deliver it immediately in person. The wax seal had made it impossible for Dr. Palliser to open it during the carriage ride. Dr. Palliser loved secrets when he could lord them over others and hated them with the same passion when he was not allowed to be part of them.

Dr. Palliser offered the box. Reverend Terwillegar accepted the package and set it on his desk, carefully avoiding the ink-drenched sermon papers. He sat behind his desk and looked expectantly at his guest.

This, too, irritated Dr. Palliser. He hoped that Reverend Terwillegar would open it in his presence. Trying to spur the nervous twit into action, Dr. Palliser spoke again. "I suggest you wash your hands immediately after we see what's inside," he said. "It came from the leper's abode."

"I beg your pardon?"

Dr. Palliser sighed, making it appear he thought Reverend Terwillegar was dense. The sigh, however, came because Reverend Terwillegar had not taken the hint and begun to open the package.

"The leper's abode," Dr. Palliser repeated.

"You found where he lived!"

"Not I." Dr. Palliser dusted his immaculately manicured hands, as if above the investigative work himself. "We received your note yesterday indicating that the man had lived above a pub. The archbishop had a discreet conversation with the commissioner of the Metropolitan Police Force. Large as this city might be, the resources available to the commissioner were ample to find out last night which pub had the singular distinction of renting a room above the premises to a man who claimed to be so badly burned he would not venture out in public."

"The archbishop did this?" An innocent in politics, it had not occurred to Reverend Terwillegar that the archbishop's power extended so far into the secular world.

"Naturally," Dr. Palliser said. "Despite Dr. Cuplinn's assurances to the contrary, an epidemic of leprosy is something to be highly feared. We——" Before coughing, Dr. Palliser heavily emphasized the word *we,* thus unnecessarily aligning himself again with the power of the archbishop. Then Dr. Palliser coughed, giving him the chance to repeat the *we,* as in he and the archbishop. *"We* needed to confirm there were no other lepers. And, of course, we needed to disinfect where this leper had lived."

Reverend Terwillegar nodded with understanding. Yes, this was why the archbishop had sent him to the leper with those questions. But the commissioner himself! Who would have thought!

Fascinated by the turn of the conversation, he had completely forgotten the package or why it might matter to him.

Dr. Palliser coughed again and smoothed back his hair. "The package . . ."

"Oh yes, the package." Flustered by the presence of Dr. Palliser, Reverend Terwillegar was unable to think clearly and misinterpreted Dr. Palliser's impatient hint. "Let me take care of this."

Reverend Terwillegar stood again and dug into his pocket, staining his pants with the last of the ink on his hands. He found a few coins and offered them to Dr. Palliser as a tip.

Startled, Dr. Palliser accepted the money before realizing that Reverend Terwillegar assumed he had requested a tip, like some common deliveryman. Worse, some of the ink on the coins had now transferred to his own hands.

"Thank you so very much," Reverend Terwillegar said, unaware of Dr. Palliser's sudden fury. "And what was the archbishop's decision on the baby girl?"

"Foundling hospital," Dr. Palliser snapped.

"Foundling hospital?"

As a point of fact, the archbishop had wanted time to give the matter more consideration, and Dr. Palliser had just now made this decision for the archbishop. He often did this when dealing with people who would never go to the archbishop directly.

"But isn't anyone worried about contagion? After all, this baby has been in contact with a leper."

Because he'd made his decision in a moment of extreme irritation, Dr. Palliser had not considered this but was not about to change his mind, especially since making it appear it had been the archbishop's decision. "She must be kept in a separate room, away from the other foundling children."

"For three years? Day and night?"

"Heaven's sakes, man, what are you talking about?" Dr. Palliser never liked to be second-guessed, and certainly not by a mouse of a clergyman with ink on his forehead.

"It takes up to three years for any leprous symptoms to appear," Reverend Terwillegar explained, remembering what he had learned the day before.

"Don't tell me things I already know," Dr. Palliser said. He did not want to seem ignorant of the medical matters of leprosy. "She will be quarantined for three years then."

"That seems a bit harsh," Reverend Terwillegar said.

"Shall we ship her to a colony and let her die there like the leper, even if she is untouched now by the disease?"

Reverend Terwillegar blinked at the callousness of that remark. "Certainly not. But three years locked in a room, and her being such a young child seems—"

"Are you casting doubt on the archbishop's decision?"

"No. No."

"Good then. See that it is done."

With an imperious wave, Dr. Palliser began to stroll out of Reverend Terwillegar's office. He stopped.

"Oh yes, as I mentioned, Dr. Cuplinn awaits. The archbishop dispatched him with me to inspect your lepers. Have no fear, this physician has been cautioned to the greatest secrecy. When he has finished with his duties, find him another carriage. I have pressing matters and will not wait here for him."

One more imperious wave, and Dr. Palliser departed, with none of his irritation dissipated.

It bothered Dr. Palliser far more that he had not discovered what was in the package than that he had just condemned a baby to three years of solitude.

REVEREND EDWARD TERWILLEGAR looked at the sealed package briefly. While he had some curiosity, he dreaded more the prospect of touching anything that had been in possession of a leper.

While he debated the merits of opening the package, another knock interrupted him. He looked up to see a short, redheaded man at his door.

"You'll be Reverend Terwillegar?" the man asked in a thick brogue.

"Yes."

"Dr. Cuplinn. And I prefer not to waste time."

"Oh yes." Reverend Terwillegar placed the package under his desk. Later, he would forget about it completely.

MISS HOGG'S APPEARANCE out of doors with Gabrielle proved
to be a spectacle for the other women.

They all knew, of course, that Miss Hogg had taken on the
duty of caring for the leper baby. They all knew, too, that Miss
Hogg had been taking the utmost precautions to avoid contamination by contact with the leper baby. A few had even seen Miss
Hogg in her wraps of linen and had immediately passed on this
gossip.

But here in the morning sun was the first time that any saw
the leper baby and Miss Hogg's mummylike appearance.

For Ima had decided that it was unfair to leave Gabrielle in
the attic all day. Not with the stretch of glorious weather that had
blessed all of London.

In private with Gabrielle, Ima would have been unwrapped.
She craved Gabrielle's touch and loved it when Gabrielle reached
up to explore Ima's face with her tiny fingers.

This, however, was not private. Ima knew she needed to keep
up appearances; as she carried Gabrielle to a stretch of manicured
grass, she sweated heavily beneath the linen wraps. Still, out here
in wraps was better than in the attic without. Especially for Gabrielle, who tottered and staggered as she continued to experiment
with walking.

Ima clapped with glee as she watched Gabrielle's happy curiosity. First the grass, when Gabrielle pulled loose and tried to eat it.
Then Gabrielle's pursuit of a butterfly. Her quizzical stares at the
flowers nearby. And another attempt to eat, this time the blossoms.

Again and again, Ima laughed aloud, unaware of the stares and surprise it drew from the women who made it a point to pass by and look at the leper baby, as if Gabrielle were an attraction at an exhibit.

They were surprised to see a leper baby appear so normal.

And more surprised at Ima's laughter.

They'd never heard it before.

# 15

REVEREND TERWILLEGAR approached the leper's shed with Dr. Cuplinn, who carried a leather satchel in one hand, with his folded jacket resting in his other hand. The reverend was ready with his heavily perfumed handkerchief. He put it to his nose as they approached.

As their shadows—all that much darker because of the cloudless blue sky and bright sun—hit the door that kept the leper locked inside, Dr. Cuplinn grabbed Reverend Terwillegar's shoulder and pulled him back from unlatching the lock with the hand that did not press his handkerchief in place.

"Do you smell that?" Dr. Cuplinn whispered.

Reverend Terwillegar shook his head, keeping the handkerchief firmly in place. He had offered another perfumed hankie to the physician earlier. It was not his fault the physician had not accepted.

"Leave the door alone and come with me," Dr. Cuplinn instructed with no pretense at politeness. His wild red hair seemed to blaze in the June sun. Dr. Cuplinn set his leather satchel down beside the door and marched to the shade of a tall oak.

Reverend Terwillegar, much puzzled, followed the physician. "Yes?" he asked.

"Were it not for my oath to heal, I would punch you squarely in the nose," Dr. Cuplinn said. His intense blue eyes did not blink as he glared at Reverend Terwillegar. "How long has that man been kept in there?"

Reverend Terwillegar did blink. Repeatedly. He felt the physician's anger. "Since . . . since his arrival. Three days prior."

"Is he a beast? livestock?" Dr. Cuplinn's voice rose. "No. Surely not. For you would have treated a cow or pig better than you have this man. Look about you!"

Bewildered, Reverend Terwillegar tried to understand what the physician meant with his waving arms. "I see nothing."

"Nothing? You must be blind. I see flowers. I see blue sky. I see butterflies on rose petals, and I see swallows dipping and swooping. These estate grounds are glorious, and days of such outstanding warmth are too rare to be wasted."

"Yes, but—"

"And you have a man locked in darkness. For three days now. Have you no compassion?"

"Please." Reverend Terwillegar hated confrontation. "The archbishop sent you here. He must have explained it all. That man has leprosy. I am carrying out the archbishop's instructions. He agreed the man must be kept separate in order to—"

"The archbishop has seen where you keep this man?"

"No. It was the best we could think of. It seems of utmost urgency to quarantine the leper to prevent others from—"

"The leper? Is that how you protect your callousness? By thinking of him as an object? A leper? He is a man, no different than you and I. What is his name?"

"It . . . I . . . he has not offered, nor did I think to ask."

"Stand back, Reverend, for if you remain within reach, most surely shall I strike you, man of God or not."

Reverend Terwillegar wisely obeyed.

"You never bothered to ask his name. And what have you offered this dying man for comfort in his last days?"

"Dying?"

"I did not understand your handkerchief until the whiff of gangrene reached me at the door. That is why I removed us to the shade of this tree. You think I wanted to discuss that poor man's condition within his earshot?"

"Gangrene. Oh dear."

"Oh dear?" Dr. Cuplinn was momentarily speechless as he considered Reverend Terwillegar. "You thought that was the odor of leprosy?"

Reverend Terwillegar meekly nodded. "That explains, I suppose, why the smell worsened so quickly."

"Hold me back, dear Lord," Dr. Cuplinn said, upward to the sky. "Hold me back." The physician took a few deep breaths. "May I speculate?" Dr. Cuplinn asked with great civility. He did not wait for Reverend Terwillegar's permission. "Did you perhaps receive your position here because of family influence?"

"It's not uncommon," Reverend Terwillegar protested, lulled by Dr. Cuplinn's composure. "The Church of England fills its churches by—"

"You're from a wealthy family then?"

Reverend Terwillegar blinked again. This time from surprise at the physician's vulgarity. The well-bred did not speak of money. "What relevance does this have to—"

"May I further speculate, then, that you went from the bosom of your mother to the bosom of the church, well protected from the ugliness of this great world."

"Most definitely not. I spent years at Oxford. The rigors of the academic life are well documented. I—"

"Coddled first by your mother, then by academia, then by the church. I invite you, Reverend Terwillegar, to spend a week with me. On the streets among the poor. Among the dying and the diseased. Hold the hand of a mother who has just lost a child. Or speak to a father who has lost his wife in childbirth. Listen to their wails of anguish. Try to comfort their pains and hungers."

"Yes, yes," Reverend Terwillegar said, anxious to please this firebrand of passion in front of him.

"Yes, yes?" Dr. Cuplinn thundered. "You have no comprehension of what I mean. You believe you serve the Christ here? Or is your title simply a comfortable position that gives you respect you haven't earned?"

Reverend Terwillegar felt his face begin to flush. "My good man, you have no right to speak to me that way. I tend to a flock of his followers and—"

"I will speak to you any way I see fit. How can any of you call yourself followers when you lock up a man to die in isolation?"

"We—"

"Oh, shut your mouth," Dr. Cuplinn snapped. "After you bring some water to me, go elsewhere and find some women to lead in hymns. There is a man who needs help and compassion, and even though he has the misfortune of remaining in the bosom of the church, I intend to see he gets it."

"I will have to report your insolence to the archbishop." Stung, Reverend Terwillegar was pleasantly surprised to discover he could fight back. He'd never been one to stand up for himself, but he did, after all, come from an established family.

"My insolence won't surprise Palliser in the slightest. He only deals with me from necessity. All of his preferred physicians would have declined to see a leper."

Dr. Cuplinn glared one final time at Reverend Terwillegar, then marched back to the shed.

IMA SET GABRIELLE down on the grass and left her standing there.

She then walked a short distance from Gabrielle and squatted. She held her arms wide and called out the baby's name.

Gabrielle lurched forward, her beautiful round face filled with giddy joy at the simple act of walking. "Mah! Mah!" She tried to run and fell hard. She rolled twice.

"Baby!" Ima rushed to pick her up. Although Gabrielle's eyes had begun to fill with tears, she did not cry.

"Baby, baby," Ima soothed. "You'll be fine. I love you. You'll be fine. I'll make sure nothing hurts you. Understand, little one? I love you."

# 16

"PLEASE, come with me outside."

In the darkness of the interior of the shed, Nathaniel could not see the face of the man who spoke to him. Nathaniel did not fight, however, as thick, strong hands reached under his arms. He allowed himself to be lifted, and as he leaned against the man's shoulder, found himself towering over the man who held him.

"Outside?" Nathaniel croaked. The cooler air beyond the open door tantalized him.

"Let me carry your weight," the man instructed. "Slowly, move forward."

Nathaniel had been despondent and lying motionless on his side for over twenty-four hours, so long that he felt paralyzed. He could not find the energy to move. The shorter man was surprisingly strong and did not seem bothered by Nathaniel's weight. The straw rustled as the man dragged him out of the shed toward the trimmed green grass of the estate grounds. Once outside, the man set him down gently.

Nathaniel collapsed on his side again.

"Shall I help you to sit?" The man didn't wait for Nathaniel's answer but put an arm beneath Nathaniel's neck and assisted him into an upright position.

Nathaniel's eyes filled with tears against the brightness of the sun. He still could not focus on the face of the man who had helped him.

"Thank you," Nathaniel said. "Thank you so much." He was amazed at his profound gratitude. To be allowed to sit outside. What a wonderful thing.

"I have fresh water for you," the man said. "Here, drink."

Nathaniel tried to take the offered cup in his gloved hands, but he could not control his shaking. As he lifted the cup, he spilled most of the water across his cloak.

The man held the back of Nathaniel's head in one hand, and with the other, tilted the cup toward Nathaniel's mouth. Until the water reached his throat, Nathaniel had not realized how long it had been since he drank.

From beneath his hood, Nathaniel saw more of the man. His red hair. The intense blue eyes.

"What is your name?" the man asked with his Scottish brogue blurring the words.

"Have you seen Gabrielle? Is she in good spirits? Where have they taken her?"

"Gabrielle?"

"The baby."

"You know the baby's name." This was interesting. Palliser had inferred that the leper had simply delivered the baby. Yet the man's obvious concern hinted that it was more complicated than that. "I will tend to her next. But first, you. What is your name?"

"Has no one told you of my leprosy?" Nathaniel answered, astounded that this man dared to touch him. A hand behind his neck. Another, resting softly on his chest.

"Certainly. That's why I'm here. I'm a physician. George Cuplinn." It was important to the physician that he know the man's name, for the intimacy of caring for him required it. "And how, sir, may I address you?"

"You have no fear of becoming a leper yourself?"

"Yes. And of succumbing to cholera. Or the pox. Or any of a number of things sent by the devil to afflict us. But my fate is God's will. What is firmly in my control, however, is the choice to do his will. How, sir, may I address you?"

Nathaniel could not speak, for he was weeping. If this man dared touch a leper, this man would see that Gabrielle was safe. What a wonderful thing, the touch of another human.

"I'm going to redress the bandages on your ankle," Dr. Cuplinn said, allowing Nathaniel dignity by not commenting on his weeping. "After, we will find you a proper bed and feed you."

Dr. Cuplinn had noticed that two of the man's fingers were partially gone. He didn't need to guess how it had happened. He knew too well from his experience at leper colonies that rats preyed upon them during the night. Yet . . .

Dr. Cuplinn's fury rose again. Yet this would not have

happened if the man had not been left unattended in the straw of a cattle shed.

"A proper bed? I'm . . . I'm a leper."

"So you have made clear. And I'm a physician. Thus, each of us has our duties. And yours is to accept the ministration of all I can do to help. Understand?"

As Dr. Cuplinn spoke, he peeled off the pus-soaked strips of cloth around Nathaniel's ankle. Only because he had years of experience was he able to prevent a sharp and audible breath of horror.

The flesh had been mangled so thoroughly by the dog's grasp that not even the purple-and-green swelling of the tissues hid the extent of the savagery. Long splinters of the lower end of the shinbone protruded just above the ankle, and the foot itself hung only by the soft flesh and the tendons.

"You feel no pain?" Dr. Cuplinn asked as neutrally as possible. If there was any blessing in the leprosy that afflicted this poor man, this was it.

"I haven't felt pain in years. But there does seem to be a slight sensation of warmth below my knee. And, it seems, a fever takes me and leaves me at its capricious will."

*Slight warmth indeed,* Dr. Cuplinn thought.

The poison of the gangrenous infection had begun, puffing the man's lower leg with angry red. Without medical attention, he would be sure to die, and even with assistance, he faced an uphill battle for life.

"I have grim news," Dr. Cuplinn said. He had learned over the years that the best way was to not provide false hope. "Infection has set in. Your life is in peril. If we remove your foot, the more chance that you will be spared."

"I do not wish to be spared. Surely you understand that. Promise me that your efforts instead will provide for the baby Gabrielle."

Again, the intense concern for the baby, and all that it implied. Dr. Cuplinn let none of these thoughts cross his face. "You already have my promise that I will care for the child. May I remove your hood and cloak?"

"No," Nathaniel choked out. "By the love of God's mercy, no. I beg you. Spare me the shame!"

"And what," the man asked softly, "do you know of God's mercy?"

"I lost my wife and my family. I lost my health. And I've lost Gabrielle," Nathaniel said. "So until this moment, in your arms, nothing."

# 17

"YOU NEED NOT SHRINK from me like that," Dr. Cuplinn told Reverend Terwillegar, seeing the thin man's eyes widen. "I'm not here to bite your head off again."

In the doorway of Reverend Terwillegar's study, Dr. Cuplinn rubbed his eyes and sighed before continuing. "As a point of fact, I'm here to apologize for my earlier outburst."

"Apologize?" Reverend Terwillegar sat behind his desk, with a strong cup of tea to keep him company. He had his Bible open in front of him, finger resting on the passage he had been reading silently when Dr. Cuplinn coughed discreetly at the doorway.

"May I sit?" Dr. Cuplinn asked.

Reverend Terwillegar hesitated.

Again, Dr. Cuplinn sighed, correctly interpreting Reverend

Terwillegar's hesitation. "Let me assure you, I will not bring leprosy into your study. After helping the poor man, I have washed thoroughly. Besides that, you are a strong, healthy man. It is remote that even direct contact with a leper would do you any harm."

"You know this to be true?"

Reverend Terwillegar had not invited Dr. Cuplinn to sit. The smell of the tea made the lack of welcome all the more acute, and Dr. Cuplinn wistfully noticed the fresh crumpets and preserves beside a pot of tea on a side table.

Leaning against the doorway, Dr. Cuplinn spoke gently. "Reverend, it was no coincidence the archbishop sent word to me about your visitor. I've dealt with leprosy here and abroad for the last decade. Little known as I might be to the rest of London, I am a foremost expert on the subject. You would be surprised at how many lepers I have dealt with here in the city. And with all cases, like yours, those involved plead for the utmost secrecy. They, like you, fear what they don't understand. Thus, I should not have held you to blame for the terror which prompted you to treat your visitor as you did."

Dr. Cuplinn let out a deep breath. "Please, may I sit?"

Finally, Reverend Terwillegar pointed at the armchair near his desk.

"Thank you," Dr. Cuplinn said. He moved across the study and settled in the armchair. "Some tea, perhaps? For I admit, I'm a proud man, and these words of apology come easier if my throat is not parched."

"Yes, yes." Reverend Terwillegar hastily poured a cup and handed it to the physician. "But I don't understand. I'm the one who . . ."

Reverend Terwillegar pointed at the Bible. "Your rebuke cut to my heart and sent me here. I've been reading how the Christ himself dealt with lepers. I see too well that I have fallen far short of his example."

Dr. Cuplinn smiled wanly. "Point me to one man who doesn't fall far short of his example. I doubt the Christ would have stormed at you as I did."

"Your anger is much easier to justify and forgive than my neglect," Reverend Terwillegar answered. The directness of Dr. Cuplinn's gaze prompted an unexpected confession. "Indeed, there are days when I wonder if my faith is real or imagined."

"Christ lives. He is seen when we serve him by serving others."

"That, too, is what I tell others. It seems I need to learn it for myself."

"Then you will not be too disturbed when I tell you that I moved him myself to an empty room where he can get sunshine and gaze out on the grounds?"

"If you tell me there is no danger to the others."

"No danger. Later, simply to reassure the others, have the room limed."

"Later? You are taking him away soon?"

"I believe he will die soon. You could do worse than spending time with him. Give him the hope that comes with faith. He tells me he has no interest in a God who would do such damage to him."

"Yes, of course." Edward knew the words of comfort to murmur in such situations. "Tell me, if you will, how it was you became an expert on lepers."

"Greed." A wan smile. "Pure and simple greed. You see, the wars have and will continue to send us back many fine men horribly disfigured. I once dreamed that as a physician, I might make my mark and my fortune by learning the ways to repair such disfigurements. All my studies pointed to India, for there, over the last few hundred years, doctors have experimented on ways to replace the flesh lost by leprosy."

Reverend Terwillegar had his cup of tea halfway to his mouth. He stopped in midsip and studied Dr. Cuplinn to see if his statement was said in jest.

"Do you know, for example," Dr. Cuplinn said, "that the skin on one part of your body will grow in another? Oh yes. It is a painful and uncomfortable process. If I were to replace the flesh of your nose with a flap from your arm, my first surgery would require peeling it back from your arm and setting it against your face. I would have to arrange a contraption to keep your arm pressed against your face for six to eight weeks so that your blood supply allowed the skin to grow into place. Finally, a second surgery would be required to remove your arm from your face, for the skin would literally grow where directed on your nose. The final result will fool no one into believing it is the nose the person had at birth, but it is far better than two gaping holes in the middle of the face. This leper here. Surgery will not make his face perfect, but it will certainly repair it so the man can walk in public without shame."

Reverend Terwillegar remained frozen with the cup of tea poised in front of his mouth.

Dr. Cuplinn was enjoying the attention of his audience. "Methods such as this I learned directly at the feet of the most skilled surgeons in India. Unfortunately, I also learned their compassion."

"Unfortunately?" Reverend Terwillegar set his cup down, untouched.

"Quite. In the face of all the suffering I witnessed there, I lost my taste for money and fame."

Dr. Cuplinn stared briefly at the oil painting that hung above Reverend Terwillegar's desk. It showed men on horses, pursuing hounds, who in turn, pursued a lonely fox, frozen in the painting with his head turned back over his shoulder to glance at his approaching death.

"My most vivid memory is of the day I arrived at a leper colony. Some of the villagers arrived with food, which they would set down at the edge of a field. The lepers knew not to approach until the villagers walked away. And as soon as they did, they ran forth. Some on crutches. One poor man on crutches was so hungry that as he fell farther behind, he simply dropped his crutches and ran. The fact that his splintered anklebones protruded from his flesh and he was literally running on broken bone bothered him not at all."

Reverend Terwillegar turned white.

"Yes," Dr. Cuplinn said, "I had the same reaction. Still, my heart was untouched. And then——" he stared at his hands, turning them front and back——"one morning I woke up with white spots on the skin of the back of my hands. In a flash of horror, I saw that I'd contracted the very disease I had been seeking to profit from. The irony is that I knew full well what lay ahead for me. Leprosy destroys the nerve endings, you know. It isn't until you lose sensation that you realize that pain is a wonderful gift from God. It alerts us to damage done to our body. And, alongside that pain, those same nerves deliver to us the other wonderful sensations God permits us. Seeing the white spots on my hands, I realized that my body would soon begin its horrible slow destruction."

"Surely you don't—" Reverend Terwillegar actually drew back from Dr. Cuplinn.

"No. Surely I don't. The spots were a temporary affliction, the result of an unrelated skin disorder. I should have known that. Leprosy takes some time to show itself, and I'd only been there a few months. Still, it was enough of a scare that I understood what it might be like to be so cursed."

"And?"

"And I came to a profound realization. Perhaps nothing new to you, but to me, life changing. I understood then that we are no different from a leper. Like Job, he loses his wealth, his health, and his family. Like Job, he has reason to look upward and ask why God would allow such a thing. The answer is there for all of us. In the end, death will take our wealth, our health, and our family. Job was fortunate enough to finally see the great truth. When everything we believe matters is stripped away—as it surely will happen sooner or later—it is the fact that God loves us which is all we really ever had."

Dr. Cuplinn allowed a quiet smile. "I said pain is a gift. It is. With the peaks come the valleys. We must remember that this life—and all the joy and pain in it—is not our final destiny. And once I truly knew this, my life was changed. Do you understand what I am saying?"

"Yes," Reverend Terwillegar said. Although he did not intend it to be, it was still a lie.

Dr. Cuplinn rose. "I must be on my way. Thank you for your forgiveness. I will return tomorrow, for the man needs assistance, and I cannot expect you to touch him in his condition."

"Yes," Reverend Terwillegar said, very much relieved.

Dr. Cuplinn stopped at the door. "One thing. A curiosity. I sense this man is much closer to the baby than you were led to believe. I would look into his background if I were you."

"Quite," Reverend Terwillegar said, distracted by thoughts of what his next sermon might require. "As soon as possible."

That promise, like the package beneath his desk, Reverend Terwillegar forgot promptly as he turned back to his unfinished sermon.

# 18

IMA DELAYED her other duties far too long, preferring to stay outside with Gabrielle.

Finally, however, she brought Gabrielle back to the attic. Once hidden inside, she eagerly removed the linen wraps and held Gabrielle close. She sang a few more lullabies and marveled at Gabrielle's beauty and happiness. Then, reluctantly, she set Gabrielle down.

"Mah?"

"I'll be back, little one. I promise. I'll be back as soon as I can return."

"Mah?"

Ima opened the door and stepped outside the attic room. Slowly, she closed it, watching as the gap narrowed to a tiny crack. Then she opened it wide again and smiled.

Gabrielle laughed.

Ima slowly closed the door again.

Gabrielle kept her eyes on the narrowing gap, understanding this was a game.

Again, Ima opened it suddenly and smiled.

Again, Gabrielle laughed.

Ima repeated this again and again, almost drunk with the joy she'd never allowed herself to experience before. When at last she knew she could no longer delay the other duties, she gently closed the door.

And from the attic, came an unfamiliar sound. Crying from Gabrielle.

At no other time had Gabrielle been upset to see Ima leave.

And now!

The baby needed her!

Ima opened the door and stepped inside. She held Gabrielle and quieted the sobs.

"Oh, baby," she said. "Oh, baby. Oh, baby."

THE FEVER TOOK Nathaniel again. The white of the painted walls and the white of the clean sheets on his body and bandaged leg dazzled him in the sunshine that flooded through the room.

The doctor had opened a window before departing, and the songs of birds seemed to add to the sensation that Nathaniel had already died and now rested in heaven.

If he could believe in heaven.

He'd prayed the night before, in desperation and in depression, but it had almost seemed like an utterance of black despair.

"Jesus," he cried out again, seeing his wife and son and daughter appear before him in the hazy white of his disappearing sight. "Just give me my family."

With that groan, Nathaniel lapsed into unconsciousness.

"I HAVE GOOD NEWS, Miss Hogg," Reverend Terwillegar said, half trotting to catch up to Ima as she hurried across the estate grounds, "but I must say, I've had a devil of a time finding you. You've been diligently at your devotional readings, I presume. And now headed toward the sanctuary for mediation on the Word?"

Reverend Terwillegar would not have been able to guess that Ima was walking briskly to return to Gabrielle again. Ima did not have her face wrapped in linens; she had decided to not even bother with the effort anymore. Ima stopped and waited for Reverend Terwillegar with a smile across her face.

Momentarily, it put Reverend Terwillegar off balance. He'd never seen her with this expression. If he would have thought about it further, he would have admitted to himself that it was actually a very becoming smile, transforming her face completely.

"It is a beautiful day, isn't it, Reverend Terwillegar?" Ima inhaled deeply. "Smell those flowers. And how long has it been since God has favored us with blue skies for more than three days in a row?"

Reverend Terwillegar almost stepped backward in surprise. Where was Ima's perpetual simmering anger? her hatred of men?

"Yes, yes indeed," he said, biting off his stammer as he found his voice. He surveyed the rich green of the grass and the luxurious growth of leaves on the tall oaks. "It *is* beautiful."

"God is so good," Ima said. Her face, calm and gentle, reflected her emotions.

Reverend Terwillegar found himself staring. Not only because of Miss Hogg's unusual serenity. But at how the softened lines in her face permitted an interesting beauty. If she ever let her hair grow long and perhaps wore a dress with bright colors . . .

Reverend Terwillegar found himself speculating some unclergy-like thoughts.

"You said you had good news?" she asked.

"Yes," he answered quickly, glad to be pulled back to the moment. "The archbishop has made his decision. The baby is to be sent to a foundling hospital. He has decided, I am told, that she will be quarantined for several years. Alone, as it were, until they determine whether she has leprosy."

Miss Hogg brought her hand to her mouth, as if she were hiding a gasp, which she was. "Gabrielle? When?"

"Tomorrow, I suppose," Reverend Terwillegar answered, unaware, as usual, of any subtle changes in conversational flow. "I thought you might be glad to hear of this. No longer will you have to bother with feeding the child or changing the soiled clothing."

"Tomorrow." Ima's face had lost all animation.

"I was thinking," he said, "although it is a lot to ask, that perhaps it should be you to help deliver the baby there. After all, no sense in letting anyone risk contamination when you have served so ably."

"It would appear so," she said. She could hardly force the words from her mouth.

Oblivious as he was, Reverend Terwillegar thought the subject had been thoroughly dealt with, and he turned his face to the warmth of the sun. "You are so correct," he said.

"Correct?" *Gabrielle,* Ima thought. *Dear sweet Gabrielle.* Sentenced to years of quarantine in a foundling hospital. Locked alone in a room. No one to hold her. No one to sing to her. The horror of it filled Ima.

"It is a beautiful day. And God is so good."

He whistled as he walked back to his study to go over his sermon notes, thinking perhaps it was time to spend an hour explaining to the women the goodness of God and the joy of serving him wholeheartedly because of it.

# 19

IN THE THREE MONTHS that had followed his discovery of Gabrielle beneath the fishnet, Nathaniel's love for her grew. As did his despair.

The room above the pub constantly smelled of sour beer and tobacco smoke. The noise was horrible. Each night he was forced to abandon Gabrielle while he scavenged. During the day, her only glimpse of the sun came through the dim, tiny window.

Nathaniel knew he was robbing Gabrielle. Of sunlight. Of the song of birds. Of grass under her feet.

Day by day, as her trusting gaze into his ravaged face became infinitely more sweet, it also filled Nathaniel with infinite pain.

She trusted him without reservation.

Unless he did what he must, she would believe this was life.

In a room. Above a pub.

In prison.

With a freak.

So came the moment when he wrote a letter that he pinned to Gabrielle's clothing—the letter that pleaded for his brother, Edward, to care for her.

Then, with Gabrielle safe, Nathaniel intended to return to the river where death by drowning would take away his despair.

He had not, of course, foreseen the consequences of capture by the dog that belonged to the night watchman.

# 20

LATER, REVEREND EDWARD TERWILLEGAR would tell no one of the events of the dark hours of the early morning that followed the visit by Dr. Cuplinn.

Edward knew that most listeners would say what he would have claimed until that night—visions belonged to the more excitable of parishioners, those with so little faith that as they strained for outward signs of God, they took any dream or coincidence as a direct sign. Furthermore, Edward did not want to ever see listeners raise eyebrows of pitied doubt. He knew in this age of enlightenment that others would offer a simple explanation; it had been a psychological phenomenon brought on by the reading of the passage in the Gospels and the subsequent conversation with Dr. Cuplinn.

But Edward knew differently. This, too, was a reason he would never speak of the vision. There was such truth in what happened that he did not need it validated by any discussion. Nor did he want to tarnish the miracle by making it a curiosity for others.

Indeed, the passage of time would not diminish the power of what touched him that morning. Until his deathbed, the vividness of what woke him in those early hours would always seem as if it had happened only the day before.

"BAH?"

Half asleep, Gabrielle clung to Ima's neck. Her little voice reflected uncertainty; she sensed the lateness of the hour and the disruption of routine.

"Shhh, baby," Ima whispered. She held Gabrielle tight and walked toward the open door and the hallway beyond. "Shhh."

Ima had slipped into the attic room a few minutes before and had, by dim lamplight, silently watched the rise and fall of Gabrielle's chest. Such a perfect beautiful baby. It seemed to Ima that with each of Gabrielle's breaths, her own chest swelled with more love. Was this how God intended it, she wondered, that what seemed like infinite love grew more every day? And if God intended it to be thus, she could speculate in awe at how much more she would love Gabrielle in a year. In two years.

Ima imagined the days when Gabrielle grew to be a young girl, in an exquisite dress, sitting with her for tea on sunny afternoons. Or, even more satisfying to picture, rainy afternoons with a fire at their backs to keep them warm and nothing more pressing to do than read stories, each to the other with the sound of water drumming against the windows.

But Ima's dreams did not stop there. While she wished for Gabrielle to know all that ladies must know, she wanted Gabrielle someday to walk boldly in the world of men, accomplishing all that had been denied to Ima.

*Oh, love,* Ima thought. How beautiful. How astonishing and magnificent the purpose it inspired. Now Ima understood. She'd joined the church because its rules provided comfort and safety. But that was hollow and meaningless; life was meant to be lived boldly and without fear. Love gave courage. Through Gabrielle, Ima had finally realized the truth deep in Paul's first letter to the Corinthians:

> *Though I speak with the tongues of men and of angels, and have not charity, I am become as sounding brass, or a tinkling cymbal.*

> *And though I have the gift of prophecy, and understand all mysteries, and all knowledge; and though I have all faith, so that I could remove mountains, and have not charity, I am nothing.*

> *And though I bestow all my goods to feed the poor, and though I give my body to be burned, and have not charity, it profiteth me nothing.*

No, Gabrielle would not be sent to a foundling hospital, where her smile would wither in the darkness and loneliness of a three-year quarantine. Ima had firmly decided that her own future in the church mattered little compared to the life of the child she held. No price would be too great for Ima to give Gabrielle a life of hope.

"Bah." Gabrielle was beginning to wake more, and her voice reflected it.

"Shhh," Ima whispered again. "Shhh." She carried Gabrielle into the hallway, leaving behind the lamplight. Ima intended to walk the rest of the way in darkness.

Their escape had begun.

Earlier, Reverend Terwillegar had fallen asleep normally enough. No restless turning as he mentally reviewed his list of tasks ahead. No stomach pains of indigestion to bring him back to wakefulness. Just his general weariness and sense of emptiness as his usual companions into slumber.

And then . . .

With no warning or transition, he found himself on a sparsely treed hill, with evening sunlight transfused by low clouds. In the dusty heat, his tongue stuck to the roof of his parched mouth. He heard the distant braying of a donkey.

Below was a dusty road that led into a small village of low, whitewashed buildings. Directly behind was the black mouth of a cave into the hillside, with horrible moaning coming forth from the interior. And beside him, a man in ragged clothing, his face and hands and feet disfigured by white ulcers.

The two of them watched a small procession of men leave the village below.

"It's him!" the nearby man wheezed. "The Teacher! The One who heals!"

At that, Edward found himself heedlessly running down the

hillside, curious and overwhelmed by an unreasoning hope. He broke through underbrush just ahead of the procession and stopped on the road, leaning on his knees to gasp for breath.

The small procession of men stopped, except for one who continued forward, as if it were not unusual to have a madman suddenly accost him from nowhere.

Edward's lungs slowly brought him the air he needed, and he was able to straighten and look closely into this man's face.

The gaze from those eyes pierced him, eyes that seemed to hold all truths and all sadness and all joy, eyes that saw the blackness of Edward's soul and even so, loved him without condition.

*"If thou wilt,"*

Edward found himself on his knees and pleading, transfixed by the man's gaze.

*"thou canst make me clean."*

*"If thou wilt, thou canst make me clean."*

Ima froze at hearing Reverend Terwillegar's broken voice. She'd seen a dim glow ahead, the light coming from around the next corner, and she had begun to approach it cautiously with Gabrielle fallen back to sleep in her arms. But Ima had no inkling that Reverend Terwillegar would be roaming the halls this late at night.

To whom was he talking?

Curiosity was too great for Ima to resist. With Gabrielle so soundly asleep, Ima tiptoed as lightly as her bulk would allow.

She peeked around the corner.

A lamp rested on the floor beside Reverend Terwillegar. He was kneeling, reaching upward, as if an invisible apparition stood in front of him. The shadows of his arms and hands covered much of his face. Even so, Ima thought she could see tears rolling down the man's face.

Ima was mesmerized.

THE MAN IN FRONT of Edward smiled gently and knelt in front of him. His eyes did not break their gaze from Edward's.

"Master, he is a leper!" a man in the procession behind shouted. "He has broken the law by approaching us! He has no right even to speak to you!"

A leper?

Edward stretched out his hands and saw with horror that they were as hideously curled as those of the man he had left behind at the mouth of the cave above him. He looked at his sandaled feet and saw the same horrible white ulcers, the toes that had rotted to stumps.

A leper.

"Have mercy," Edward croaked, realizing with suddenness the overwhelming shame that he had been denying to himself. "If thou wilt, thou canst make me clean."

In front of him, the Master's eyes filled with tears of compassion. "I will," the Master said softly. "Be thou clean."

Then this man with the eyes of love stepped forward and touched Edward, placing his hand on the grotesqueness of Edward's face. The moment seemed to last forever, and a warmth of peace washed over Edward, cleansing the scales of shame and pettiness, filling his emptiness with infinite tranquility.

Edward wept in gratitude. The sun broke from the clouds behind the Master's head, becoming an unbearable brightness that at the same time transfixed Edward completely.

The light grew brighter so that everything around the Master fell away, and then it was only Edward, alone in the light, feeling smaller and smaller as the light grew to fill the entire universe so that he was nothing but a speck against its intensity, yet at the same time he felt stronger and stronger until . . .

He woke.

The light still filled his eyes.

It was the light of a lamp. Which sat on the floor beside him.

And he realized he was kneeling in the hall.

Alone. In his nightclothes.

Far from the bed where he had laid his head to sleep.

IMA CONTINUED TO STARE as Reverend Terwillegar pleaded to an empty spot in front of him. Briefly, she forgot that Gabrielle was in her arms. Briefly, she forgot that Reverend Terwillegar was blocking her escape.

As she watched, Reverend Terwillegar's entire body shuddered, and a great sob escaped his mouth. Moments later, he opened eyes shiny with tears and seemed to stare right at her.

After a brief hesitation, he rose to his feet and took an uncertain step in her direction.

With Gabrielle in her arms, Ima fled back toward the attic room.

FILLED WITH THE GLOW of a love from beyond, Edward felt that he now saw not with his eyes but with his heart.

He hurried from the hallway to the room that held the man with leprosy. He hung the lamp above the man's bed and now held him, cradling his back with one arm to help the man sit upright. Unlike before, the smell of gangrene deterred Edward not the slightest, nor did the man's gnarled fingers, ulcerated forearms, and disfigured face.

With his free hand, Edward dampened a cloth in a bucket of cold water, then gently wiped the man's forehead. The man was unconscious with fever, moaning as he ground his teeth.

How could he not have seen this man's pain earlier? Edward wondered. How could he have been so blind to another soul in such need of compassion?

"Oh, dear Lord," Edward prayed aloud, "please forgive me for my sins. Please be with this man in his darkest hour."

Edward continued to dampen the man's face, wringing the cloth to make it cool, wiping away the great beads of heavy sweat on the man's forehead.

*Is it too late?* Edward asked himself. *Will this man die without knowing the touch of the Christ?*

*The touch of the Christ.*

Edward reflected on the vision and savored the warm peace that had not diminished in the slightest since he'd woken in the hallway with a lamp in his hand. He understood that the past was exactly that. The past. He'd been touched by the Christ, touched by the infinite love of his creator. With this cleansing love, there was no need to try to cling to the regrets and shame that had been removed by that touch. Trite murmurings of comfort belonged to the past. As did the role of a dignified clergyman above the fray of pain and sorrow and blood and anguish. Christ himself, from the heights of glory, had descended to immerse himself unflinchingly in all of what afflicted mankind—comforting those in mourning, healing the sick, and, yes, reaching out to lepers. This was part of love, sharing in another's pain. Edward had the ultimate example, and from this moment forward he would follow.

Thus, for Edward, cleansed by the touch of the Master, now it was the present that mattered. And what lay ahead.

Beginning with what Edward could do to help the man in his arms.

Although the man's eyes were closed, Edward spoke to him. Quietly. Edward told the man about the healing touch of the living Christ. Edward spoke to the man of the things he'd only repeated before as a clergyman should, not truly understanding them himself. Until the touch. Edward told the man about the peace that came with reaching for the Christ, how all shame burned away in the greatness of that light that shone from him. Edward told the man about meaning, how the understanding of God's love had given Edward purpose, the desire to show this love to others. Edward told the man about hope, that death might strip him of everything yet was the gateway to something much greater than life.

It seemed to Edward that the man became calmer. His eyes remained closed, the sweat still beaded, yet the gnashing of teeth stopped. As did the nearly inaudible moans of pain.

In the lamplight, Edward began to unbutton the man's shirt, intending to place the damp cooling cloth on his chest. He saw, on the man's skin yet to be ravaged by leprosy, a birthmark. Below his collarbone, on his right shoulder. Reddish brown, the size of a man's palm, roughly star shaped.

The sight of the birthmark transfixed Edward. Edward knew this birthmark.

"My brother," Edward whispered, "it is you."

IMA SPENT THE REST of the night in the attic room, holding Gabrielle, who continued to sleep with soft snores that would have amused Ima in any other circumstance.

Ima, however, was too agitated, thinking first how foolish she had been. Desertion with Gabrielle during the dark of night with no real plans had been a desperate reaction to the news that Gabrielle must be sent to the foundling hospital. What if Ima had made it away from the grounds safely? She would have been forced to travel through London at night, past the Irish tenements. To where? She'd thought earlier that she would walk the streets until her banker's office opened, upon which she would apply there for enough money to buy passage for two on any ship away from England. What if she'd been accosted by criminals?

And now, thinking more carefully, she also saw other flaws in her earlier, hasty plan.

To appear at the bank with a baby in her arms would certainly raise questions. Especially with the money she had intended to withdraw from the ample accounts that until now she'd found no reason to access. It would not take long for pursuing authorities to learn of her whereabouts. Nor to find out on which ship she had sought to secure passage. Their eventual capture would have been certain.

And—she hated thinking of it—what if Gabrielle did carry leprosy? Not that Ima worried for herself; she'd made her decision to accept the risk on the day she'd removed the linen wraps from her face. But there were others on their journey that Ima would have exposed to the danger through Gabrielle. It was not right, Ima knew, to inflict the disease on so many innocents, even if Gabrielle herself had been an innocent who should never have been touched by leprosy.

Thus was the blessing that Reverend Terwillegar had been there to stop her.

It forced her to plan more carefully.

Which she did.

By dawn, she knew what needed to be done to protect Gabrielle. And she was willing to pay the price.

THE TIME OF NIGHT did not matter to Edward.

In his study, with the lamp's oil burning low, he sat at his desk, hunched over the contents of the now unsealed package from the archbishop.

Edward understood why the archbishop had had it delivered to him in such a manner. And Edward understood so much more.

He sat there awake and unmoving long after the lamplight died.

And at dawn, he knew what he had to do to protect his Nathaniel. And he was willing to pay the price.

AT THE BELLS that marked first prayers, Ima left Gabrielle in the attic and hurried to find Reverend Edward Terwillegar.

AT THE SOUND of those same bells, Reverend Edward Terwillegar left his study and hurried to find Miss Ima Hogg.

# 21

"I BELIEVE THIS DRESS IS PERFECT," Ima told the shopkeeper, a man her age wearing a drab black suit. "See how the blue brings out the blue of her eyes."

He was a dour man, the shopkeeper, with a bald skull and massive lamb-chop sideburns. Despite his predisposition, he smiled in agreement with Ima. Gabrielle had captivated him over the previous half hour, giggling and cooing as Ima tried one dress on her, then another.

"You've good taste," he told Ima. "And I doubt I've seen bigger blue eyes my entire life."

Ima beamed in return. Had she known shopping could be this enjoyable, why, she'd have begun the habit years earlier.

Gabrielle looked adorable.

The dress was blue velvet, and a light blue ribbon decorated her curling wisps of hair. She wore tiny white shoes and white stockings. Every time Ima set her on the floor, Gabrielle would walk in her drunken sailor steps, giggling with glee at her newfound ability to lurch from one corner of the shop to the other. Ima's difficulty was in containing Gabrielle; Ima had to be careful that Gabrielle did not make direct contact with the shopkeeper. Twice already he had tried to pick her up. For Ima, the joy of this occasion was tinged by the sadness that came with the reason for her carefulness.

"That's it then?" the shopkeeper asked.

"Yes, that's it."

"But what about you?"

"Me?"

"Ma'am, with all respect, the clothes you wear hardly seem fitting for the company of such a baby, and—" the shopkeeper looked down at his shoes—"your own smile is so pretty that . . ."

"Good sir!" Ima said, shocked. Not at his forwardness. But in surprise. She blushed. At least, she thought it was a blush. No one had ever complimented her before, so she was not familiar with the sensation.

The shopkeeper's comment was no idle compliment to ensure that Ima spent more money. It had become true. The inner fire of love had done something to Ima's exterior. When she smiled, it lit her eyes with new liveliness and transformed her once perpetual harshness into something attractive.

"Forgive me," he said. He had surprised himself with the comment.

"Nothing to forgive," Ima said. "And, had I more time, I

would consider new clothing. But I have a carriage waiting on the street."

"Pressing business?"

Ima nodded as she scooped up Gabrielle. "Yes, we are off to Westminster. To see the archbishop."

"Bah," Gabrielle said firmly.

MIDMORNING, Nathaniel woke during one of the spells when his fever lessened.

He turned his head slightly on his pillow, and too weak to sit, he saw white ceiling and white walls, glowing with the sunlight that had never fully pierced the grimy, small window of the room above the pub, where daylight had always kept him prisoner since his return to London. He looked down briefly. With his arms and legs and body beneath the white sheets, he saw nothing of himself. He could almost believe his leprosy had disappeared. Although his throat ached for water, he felt rested. More importantly, he felt clean for the first time that he could remember since stepping off the ship at the London docks five years earlier. Instinct told him he would die soon; here, in sunshine, with fresh air coming through an open window, with the songs of birds drifting inside, it would be a good place to die. He was ready.

"My brother," he heard a voice say as he stirred. "It is you."

Nathaniel turned his head to the opposite side of the bed, toward the voice from Edward, who was sitting near the bed.

"My brother?" Nathaniel asked. Had he mumbled during his fever, telling his dreadful secret?

Their eyes met. In that moment, Nathaniel's shame returned to him. This was his brother, looking at him fully in the face and seeing the hideous disfigurement with no hooded cloak to hide it from the world. Nathaniel quickly turned his head away.

"My brother," Edward repeated.

Nathaniel sensed rather than felt a soft touch on his cheek. It was the touch of Edward's hands, gently attempting to pull Nathaniel back toward him.

"No!" Nathaniel croaked.

"As you wish." Edward spoke kindly.

Nathaniel heard the chair scrape backward as Edward stood. Nathaniel had questions but could not bear to face Edward. Nathaniel clenched his jaws, waiting for Edward to leave the room.

Edward remained.

Edward lifted the sheets from Nathaniel's leg and silently began to unwrap the dressing around the swollen, gangrene-filled ankle.

"BAH?" Gabrielle saw a new face and smiled her special happy welcome, hoping to get a smile in return.

Dr. Palliser looked up impatiently from behind his desk. He'd known a woman and child were standing in the doorway but had hoped they would move on. His Westminster office overlooked the gardens where a few days earlier Dr. Palliser had met Dr. Cuplinn out of doors to assure himself he would not be tainted by a man who dealt with lepers. Arched windows let sunlight stream across Dr. Palliser's custom-built walnut desk and cabinets, playing across the large rubies of his heavy ring.

"Bah?"

Ima stood in the doorway, with Gabrielle in her arms, waiting for the man to rise.

He didn't.

"I would like to briefly see the archbishop," Ima told Dr. Palliser, shifting Gabrielle's weight. They had enjoyed the carriage ride from the shop, with Ima pointing out all the sights of London and explaining each one to Gabrielle. As if she were her own daughter.

"I don't believe you have an appointment," Dr. Palliser told Miss Ima Hogg.

Ima studied the tall, thin man and his arrogant handsomeness to see if he recognized her. Nothing in his face gave any indication.

She was accustomed to reading people. Those who knew of her wealth hid their disdain for her appearance and replaced it with false cheerfulness. Those who did not know judged her solely by her appearance and by her drab clothing, and treated her accordingly. Except for the shopkeeper an hour earlier. Ima still glowed from his compliment.

In Dr. Palliser's face, she saw only boredom. To him, she felt she was nothing more than a piece of furniture.

"It is an important matter," Ima said. "He will find it worth his while."

"As I'm sure you can understand, the archbishop is a very busy man. Perhaps if you might tell me the nature of your request and return later with your husband . . ."

He hadn't even opened his appointment book to see if she was expected. Merely gave her that smile of superior pity. As if a mere woman could not speak of serious matters unless a man guided her.

"I have no husband."

"I see." He arched his eyebrows, and that spoke enough to her. *A woman with a baby but no husband?* "Personal matters are something I expect you should take to your clergyman."

"Not this matter. Please find the archbishop for me." Dr. Palliser's scorn did not bother her. Ima now felt freedom. During her journey here, especially after the shopkeeper, she'd forgotten to be sensitive about how others judged her appearance. She loved Gabrielle and Gabrielle loved her. Appearance meant little in comparison to the wonder of this love.

*"You* are telling me what to do. Let me assure you, Miss—"

Dr. Palliser cut himself short as Ima stepped forward and placed Gabrielle on his desk.

"You cannot do that!"

"Certainly I can. She loves papers."

"Bah!" Gabrielle swept a pile of papers with one hand. With her other, she clutched at a bottle of ink.

In self protection, Dr. Palliser stood and lifted Gabrielle. He held her under her arms and lifted her toward Ima.

"Don't be afraid of her," Ima said, stepping away. "She is your daughter."

"My . . . my . . . daughter!" Dr. Palliser sputtered. As he held her, Gabrielle kicked her feet and laughed as she continued to dangle in the air. "How ridiculous!"

"Perhaps. Or perhaps not. But unless you find the archbishop immediately, that is the claim I will make. I believe it will be less troublesome for you to do as I request than to deny the allegation."

Dr. Palliser sneered. "A frivolous allegation. One look at you and anyone would know it to be a lie. To suggest that I would consort with . . ."

"With someone as ugly as I?"

"If you wish to phrase it thus."

Ima smiled. No insult could penetrate the joy now provided to her by love. "Did I claim to be the mother? I merely said this baby was yours. Do you want to speculate as to who sent me?"

She had intended it to be a bluff, of course. A simple threat to get an audience with the archbishop. So she was amazed at Dr. Palliser's reaction. The sudden paleness of his face. And his absolute, brief, stunned silence.

"That is not my daughter," he said when he found the strength to speak. "I would have known earlier."

*This is interesting,* Ima thought. *Finally, a weapon against this man.*

"It is not your daughter," Ima said. "But unless you arrange an immediate audience with the archbishop—"

"Bah!" Gabrielle said, reaching for his neck. "Bah, bah, bah."

Dr. Palliser unsuccessfully fended off Gabrielle's advances. He looked over Gabrielle's shoulder and spoke to Ima. "Yes. An immediate audience. And who shall I say is here to visit?"

# 22

"I HAVE READ YOUR DIARIES," Edward said. "They were found in your room and delivered to me by the archbishop. Most unfortunate that all those years ago you were robbed in the manner you were."

"It happens. I traveled a road in India I should not. I was waylaid, left for death. I woke in a leper's cave. They had made the difficult decision: Let me die. Or help me and risk giving me their dreaded disease. I was among them and in such a weak state, unconscious, for far too long." Nathaniel managed a smile. "It was the same decision I made for Gabrielle."

"Yet you brought her here."

"When I realized how unfair it was to raise her. Nor did I think I would put anyone here at risk. Ask Dr. Cuplinn. He tells me only the unhealthy, the weak, the starving now contract leprosy. Gabrielle is a strong, healthy baby."

"Ah yes." Despite himself, Edward smiled. "Dr. Cuplinn. Quite the man. I believe him too."

"Otherwise you would not be tending me." No bitterness in Nathaniel's voice. A simple comment. "Yesterday you feared me as . . . well . . . the plague."

"Except for Dr. Cuplinn," Edward agreed, "I would not be here. But not for the reason you imagine." Edward was reluctant to speak of the vision, even to his brother. He changed the subject.

"Along with the diaries, I have also read the letters you left to be discovered after your death and delivered to Suzanne," Edward said. "I understand you intended to throw yourself in the Thames after leaving Gabrielle with us. You have suffered much, and I only wish I had been the kind of brother who had earned enough trust that you would have allowed me to help much sooner than this. I was such a fool that I never even wondered about the letter attached to the baby, never considered it might be you."

"Why are you doing this?" Nathaniel asked, choking back anguish and renewed shame.

"Your ankle is infected," Edward answered. "Surely you know that. Your only chance at life is to keep it clean."

"I meant why are you speaking of Suzanne? To torment me just a few days before her marriage to another?"

"I have no wish to torment you, Nathaniel." Edward spoke as he dropped the heavy pus-soaked bandage in a pan on the floor.

"Then I beg you. Tell her nothing of this. Ever. Show her my letters and let her believe I died in the river as I had intended. Keep this secret and let her marry. Ensure her well-being and that of my children. Take Gabrielle and raise her as one of yours. Make me these promises and I will die a happy man."

"I cannot." Edward began to wrap clean linens around the leg, taking care not to apply too much pressure, remembering as well as he could the instructions from Dr. Cuplinn.

"You cannot?"

"About Gabrielle I can do little. The archbishop has made his decision. Gabrielle will be raised in a foundling hospital. If I defy the archbishop, it will do Gabrielle no good, for wherever I might take her, the authorities will follow. No one will risk an outbreak of leprosy upon the populace of London. But Miss Hogg has promised to do everything possible to help the child. And Miss Hogg is a considerable force. I believe there is much reason to hope for Gabrielle."

Nathaniel groaned his anguish. "The baby brought none of this upon herself."

"Nor did you bring upon yourself the fate of leprosy. Certain things we cannot change."

"And certain things you can. Honor my other request, then. Keep this secret from Suzanne."

"Nor that can I promise." Edward finished with the wrappings. He walked around to the side of the bed where he was able to face Nathaniel squarely. He met Nathaniel's eyes without showing pity or revulsion.

"You speak of compassion," Nathaniel said, "and yet deny my dying wish."

"Who says you will die?"

"I'm not a fool. This is gangrene. Nor do I have the will to live. Wait then, until I am dead, to tell Suzanne."

"She is to marry in three days. She must be allowed to choose with full knowledge of what has happened to you."

Edward stared long and hard into Nathaniel's eyes. He was accustomed to the dark hole where the nub of nose was missing. The sight no longer repulsed him. Dr. Cuplinn's words echoed in Edward's mind. *"Surgery will not make his face perfect, but it will certainly repair it so the man can walk in public without shame."*

"Do not tell her!"

"Your letters and diaries have already been sent by carriage."

"No," Nathaniel moaned. "Have you told her I am alive?"

"Not yet. I intended to do so when I visit her later today."

"Then let her believe I died by my own hand as I promised in my farewell letter."

"This is your wish?"

"This is my wish."

Edward sighed. "I shall do as you request."

DR. PALLISER LED IMA and Gabrielle farther into the interior of the building, to a surprisingly sparse study near the library. The only decoration, if it could be called that, was the archbishop's vestments hanging neatly over a chair. A tray with a fresh pot of tea had been set on his desk.

The archbishop stood waiting for their arrival. Dr. Palliser preceded them into the archbishop's study.

"Miss Hogg," he said, "I am delighted." His smile showed his delight to be genuine.

Ima had met the archbishop only one time before, during the

audience when he considered her proposal for the first women's commune in the history of the Church of England. His short dark hair was streaked with gray, and he had a neatly trimmed goatee. He was a surprisingly small man for such a supreme authority, with surprisingly elegant hands, which he extended to greet her.

Ima pretended to fumble with Gabrielle so she could not accept the clasp of his hands.

"Please," the archbishop said after a moment of awkward silence, "sit."

Still standing, Ima passed Gabrielle to Dr. Palliser, who, in the presence of the archbishop, saw no choice but to accept the baby in his arms again. While Ima guessed Dr. Palliser would remain, if only to be assured Ima made no allegations about Gabrielle's parentage, she wanted to be sure he stayed in the study with her and the archbishop.

"What a beautiful child!" the archbishop exclaimed, moving toward Dr. Palliser. "Dr. Palliser tells me you brought her today to be blessed."

*That confirms it,* Ima thought with a hidden smile. Dr. Palliser *will* remain here the entire audience to make sure I don't disagree with his falsehood.

"May I hold her?" the archbishop asked.

Ima stepped between the archbishop and his assistant and gently took the archbishop's elbow to guide him toward the pot of steeping tea.

"If you would," she said, "it seems that more and more soot hangs in the air these days, and there is no better cure for a dry throat than tea."

"Of course, of course." While surprised at Ima's straight-

forwardness—especially her hand on his elbow—the archbishop
was far too polite to comment or protest.

As he poured the tea, Ima sat. Dr. Palliser remained standing,
obviously uncomfortable with a baby now snuggled against his
neck.

"I know your time is extremely valuable," Ima said as the
archbishop handed her a cup, "so I shall come straight to the
point. I am here to convince you to rescind your decision about
the women's commune."

"Rescind? But as I recollect, you were most insistent that it be
established. Far more insistent than necessary, I might add, for I
was in total agreement. The church needs its women. In the beginning, they were the foundation. Priscilla, for example. I pray there
comes a day when women get their due. At the very least, they
deserve a chance outside the church to vote."

Dr. Palliser gave a warning cough.

"For heaven's sakes," the archbishop said to him, "this is no
journalist. She and I can speak freely."

"I share your frustration," Ima said. She sipped her tea, letting
her words hang long enough so if one wanted, one could take it she
meant the archbishop's frustration with Dr. Palliser.

The archbishop turned a kindly, inquiring gaze on Ima. "If we
dismantle the women's commune, that will make it all the more
difficult for women in the church. Surely you know that."

"I do know that."

"And yet?"

"And yet it strikes me that worship should be more than
prayers and hymns and a life of contemplation. Noble as the idea
may seem, especially to make it possible for women who wish to

live as do the nuns of the Catholic church, I have come to realize that we must follow the example of the Christ."

The archbishop nodded, allowing Ima to continue.

"What I propose," Ima said, "is to convert the grounds into a lepers hospital."

"Mercy!" Dr. Palliser exploded. "One leper appears and—"

He stopped suddenly. When the archbishop glared, it was an effective weapon.

"I highly doubt that all of London only contains one leper," Ima said. "With all of this country's citizens who travel to our far-flung outposts of the empire? Indeed, it is my understanding that a certain Dr. Cuplinn is employed more than occasionally by this office to deal with those unfortunate souls who contract the disease."

"Yes," the archbishop said, "I have never been comfortable with our solution."

"So you agree then, a lepers hospital."

"The citizens of London would never agree!" Dr. Palliser said. "To have a colony of—"

This time he stopped abruptly because Gabrielle spit up on his expensive suit. He searched frantically for his handkerchief.

"He makes a point," the archbishop said.

"I doubt we need name it a lepers hospital. The grounds are secluded. People already believe it is a monastery of sorts. It would be a simple matter to fence the grounds more fully and maintain the privacy."

"I wish it were that simple. The Reverend Terwillegar was given that post because of . . ." The archbishop sighed. "Even within the church, politics have too much sway. The Terwillegar family has supported the church for generations, in a very substantial way. I must consider all the good that is done through their donations. Edward Terwillegar has a position there ideally suited to his temperament, which also happens to keep his family content. How could I explain a sudden decision to uproot him from there?"

"Edward wishes to make the same decision," Ima said.

Palliser snorted, even as he dabbed at his jacket with his handkerchief. "Edward? He wants his tea and crumpets at the same time every day. He wants to be able to deliver his dry boring sermons to the same captive audience every Sunday. He would never agree to surrounding himself with revolting lepers."

"Enough!" the archbishop said sharply. "Each of us is called differently to serve within the body of the church. You, for example, are an administrator beyond compare. But I have not asked you to be my advisor."

Dr. Palliser set his jaw in a grimace of silent fury.

Ima set her tea aside and fumbled through her purse. She handed the archbishop a letter from Edward. As the archbishop read it, Ima stood and walked to Dr. Palliser. She took Gabrielle from him and hugged her close.

"Bah," Gabrielle said.

"Ah," the archbishop said. "This does change things, doesn't it?"

"EXCEPT FOR RECENT EVENTS, it appears to me that you took extremely good care of yourself. My guess is that you examined your hands and feet every day to ensure there were no wounds that would fester."

Nathaniel forced a smile on his face as he answered Cuplinn. "You, sir, are to be thanked for that. What I could read of leprosy was ascribed to you. I followed all the advice you offered in the medical journals."

"Because you had reason."

"My wife and children were enough reason for me to be intensely interested and concerned in learning as much as I could." Nathaniel did not know when his fever would return. He was thirsty but lucid. "My brother, as you explained, informed you of my diaries. It was and is my hope they will read my journal entries and understand what I did until I knew they would be cared for by the man who would become her husband and their father. When that day happened, I found Gabrielle and delayed ending my life. For her, too, I needed to keep my health."

"Implying that now you are finished with life?"

"I want to be. I have been promised that there is a woman who will care for Gabrielle regardless of the circumstances. As for my own family, Suzanne will have a husband shortly. He will see that they live well."

"Let me return to my point. You have taken good care of your-self. I believe we can conquer this fever and the gangrene. You will live for years if you so wish."

"I am a leper."

"And I am a foremost expert on the disease. I have learned surgery techniques that will reduce the deformity of your features. You can live a good life with your family. If you have the desire."

"I am a leper," Nathaniel said. "I am not worthy of their love."

THE ARCHBISHOP set Edward Terwillegar's letter on his desk and, still standing, sipped his own tea.

He spoke softly to Ima. "Despite the position given to me within the Church of England—or perhaps because of it—I am all too aware of how badly I fall short in God's eyes. So I am not eager to trust my own judgment. I have discovered, too, that God's will shall always be done despite the efforts of men. So, even as archbishop, I meddle in the lives of others as little as possible."

He smiled. "So when I do meddle, it is rewarding, on occasion, to see this meddling bear fruit. This truly is a blessing." He picked up the letter and reread it silently.

Dr. Palliser could bear his curiosity no longer and found a way to inquire. "Is it a matter which I must act upon for you?"

"I doubt it," the archbishop said, not unkindly. "It would appear that Edward Terwillegar no longer wishes to remain in a harbor safe from life's storms. He, too, wishes to begin London's first lepers hospital."

"Edward Terwillegar?" Dr. Palliser said with disbelief.

Ima enjoyed the warmth of Gabrielle against her chest. Gabrielle had finally become sleepy and settled her head into the nook of Ima's neck.

"Edward Terwillegar," the archbishop said. "The package that I directed you to so urgently deliver contained the diaries of that poor leper, which were found in his room. I wondered what effect those diaries might have on the reverend. It appears my hopes and prayers were answered."

"Hopes and prayers?" Dr. Palliser had forgotten all about his customary obsequiousness.

"Sometimes you forget, Dr. Palliser, that this church is more than an organization. It is founded on hope and prayer."

Dr. Palliser bowed his head at the archbishop's rebuke.

"The poor man who threw himself on the mercy of Miss Hogg and Reverend Terwillegar," the archbishop continued, "had good reason to do so. He is Nathaniel Terwillegar, Edward's brother."

Surprise again destroyed Dr. Palliser's usual caution. "That hideous leper is a Terwillegar!"

"A man with a soul as important as yours," the archbishop answered, "and now to become the hospital's first patient."

"Perhaps the second," Ima offered.

"Second?" the archbishop echoed.

"You might recall that he brought a baby with him. Surely that poor child might remain with us instead of being locked up in a room in a foundling hospital for the next three years."

The archbishop frowned. "Three years locked up! That's like condemning the poor child to prison. I can't imagine such a thing."

"We were told that was your decision."

"Certainly not! I was waiting for Edward Terwillegar's reaction to those diaries before . . ." The archbishop stared at Dr. Palliser, letting his frown deepen until Dr. Palliser actually squirmed.

"It seemed to be such a minor matter that I did not want you troubled with it," Dr. Palliser said.

"Another human's life is a minor matter?"

To find strength against that intimidating frown, Dr. Palliser drew himself up, puffing himself with righteous dignity. "Leprosy is no minor matter. I judged it far more important to protect all who might meet the baby."

"You spoke for me."

Insofar that there was no sense in turning around, Dr. Palliser defended himself. "There are times you do not like making the difficult decisions, so, yes, I made it for you."

"Which I presume then you have done on other occasions."

"Since you must presume," Dr. Palliser said, "then the other occasions have proved my judgment to be prudent."

Ima felt like she had become invisible to the two men.

"I also defend this decision," Dr. Palliser continued, emboldened by the visible lack of anger on the part of the archbishop. "Despite what Dr. Cuplinn insists to be true about leprosy, it is a fact that little is known about this disease. If that baby remains in solitude, we are assured no one else will be exposed and contract it. Is it worth even the slightest risk that others may contract the disease by direct physical contact? Given that, the quarantine is for the best."

"I suppose you would make that decision regardless of the station of the person who might be able to spread leprosy?" Ima asked.

"Of course," Dr. Palliser answered. He had selected his position to defend and had no choice now but to argue it to the end.

Which Ima knew.

"Three years quarantine," she said, "even if it were Queen Victoria herself?"

"I'm certain, in that unlikely situation, Her Majesty would agree it was better for all and make the noble decision to seclude herself from the world."

Ima turned to the archbishop. "Sir, I am impressed at your

compassion and love. I must admit, I was prepared to try much more difficult tactics, had you not agreed to the request that came from Edward and I."

"Why am I not surprised?" the archbishop said, smiling.

"For example," Ima said, "had you not agreed, my next destination was one of the daily broadsheets. I believe a story from them about the church condemning an innocent baby to three years in a prison would have put much pressure on you."

"Yes." The archbishop kept smiling. "My only question is simple. Why? After all, Edward Terwillegar has a brother who needs help. You? All I see on the surface is a woman who is suddenly willing to give up the women's commune she fought so hard to establish."

Ima patted Gabrielle's back. "Here is my reason. This is the baby that Nathaniel Terwillegar brought with him."

"Impossible!" Dr. Palliser clutched the arms of his chair.

"I love this child," Ima said, ignoring Dr. Palliser's outburst. "I love her so much that, may God forgive me, I was even prepared to use leprosy against you. That is why, after taking great care on my journey here to prevent contact with anyone, I gave Dr. Palliser the child to hold. I intended that if she must be put into quarantine, someone here should also be forced to suffer with her. Or decide that Dr. Cuplinn is correct, that there is little risk and that the quarantine be lifted."

"This is not the baby!" Dr. Palliser was standing now. "You hold her now. You carried her here. I highly doubt that you would have willingly exposed yourself to the disease, with or without Dr. Cuplinn's mistaken advice."

"That is where you condemn yourself then," Ima said. "Not

only have I held her, but I have cared for her, kissed her, and sang to her. I am very aware of the danger it might have placed upon me and I am fully prepared to accept leprosy should I contract it, though, as Dr. Cuplinn tells me, it is highly unlikely. I fully expect to spend my next three years in very close contact with her. And, whether she has leprosy or not, years and years after."

"That, then, is your decision," Dr. Palliser said to Ima.

"And mine," the archbishop said.

Dr. Palliser's eyes widened abruptly.

"Mine," the archbishop repeated to Dr. Palliser. "I am in no position to agree or disagree with Dr. Cuplinn's assessment of the disease. Privately, I am inclined to believe him. Many work among the lepers and few contract the disease. Publicly, however, for the sake of prevention of mass hysteria, I must err on the side of safety. If, as you say, the baby should be quarantined for three years, so must those in contact with her."

The archbishop turned to Ima. "Your wish is granted," he said. "Establish the lepers hospital with Dr. Cuplinn and Edward Terwillegar. Dr. Palliser will remain there during the quarantine."

The archbishop paused. "The administrative difficulties will be immense. So I hope you will be able to put Dr. Palliser to good use over the next three years. And perhaps, God willing, in turn he'll discover some of the same of what has changed you and Edward."

ALONE AGAIN, Nathaniel slipped into his fever.

Once again, he cried a short, desperate prayer he was hardly aware of uttering. "Oh, Jesus, help me."

It was his last lucid thought before the fever brought him unconsciousness.

IN THE CARRIAGE outside the great church of Westminster, Ima held Gabrielle close.

"Baby, baby, we're going home," she whispered into Gabrielle's ear. "Together. You and I."

*Thank you, God,* Ima thought. What a sweet word. *Home.*

# epilogue

"GOOD MORNING."

Two simple words. Yet they froze Nathaniel as thoroughly as if the woman speaking those words had walked into his room and fired a derringer over his head. At the window in a chair, he did not need to turn from his view of the grounds to know who she was.

"I do hope I have the right room," the woman continued, unaware of her effect on Nathaniel. "Edward sent me here. He asked that I bring you this tea and change the dressing on your face."

Nathaniel slowly turned toward the doorway. His crutches leaned against his chair.

His ears had not lied.

It was her. Suzanne. All these years since he had held her and kissed her good-bye. The three years in India. Then the exile, watching the cottage every night. She looked more lovely, more radiant than in his memories.

She gave him a brave smile. It twisted his heart, discovering his love to be so much stronger through all these years.

"May I come in?" she asked.

Nathaniel found the strength to nod. He almost reached up and touched his head to ensure that the bandages were indeed hiding his face from her.

She set the tray down on the small table at the foot of the bed.

"Please forgive me," she said, almost shyly. "This is my first day here. I may not be good at this."

"At this?" Nathaniel's voice was hardly more than a whisper.

"Helping. Edward has graciously allowed me to join his efforts here at the hospital." Suzanne poured a cup of tea. "You . . . you can drink?"

Accepting the tea, Nathaniel nodded. Since the final stage of the operation, his face had been covered with dressings changed daily. He'd learned to eat and drink as best he could.

"Edward," he said softly. "He asked you to come here?"

Nathaniel meant this room. Where he was. The man she had married.

She interpreted his question differently. "No." She hesitated. "Edward was very surprised when I offered to help him with the new hospital. It's a long story and . . ."

She hesitated.

"Go on," Nathaniel said. *Edward had sent her to this room without telling her who was waiting?*

"You know better than me," Suzanne said after a thoughtful pause, "how Edward was instrumental in founding this hospital.

That's one of the reasons I'm here. I've seen the new joy in Edward in the few months since it began, his purpose in helping others. I selfishly want the same joy."

She gave Nathaniel another shy smile. "I'm confessing this to you, I suppose, because right now I'm so frightened."

*Edward had told her then. He'd broken his promise. She was here because of guilt or pity. He would hobble out of this room on his crutches before allowing her to unwrap his face.*

"You see," she continued, "I know I want to help. But I'm afraid of failing. I need to tell you this so that you'll forgive me for what I might do wrong. I've never met a . . . a . . ."

"A leper," Nathaniel said. No bitterness. He could understand her reluctance. It would be best if he found a way to leave before she saw his face. "I know I have the disease. You need not be embarrassed or filled with pity among us."

"Thank you. If I'm to be here as long as I intend, I need to learn that."

"As long as you intend?"

"I have a son and a daughter. We will live here on the grounds. With Edward's blessing."

"You're not afraid of leprosy?"

"A little. Even though Edward reassures me there is no need to fear. But it will help Ethan and Faith. They . . ."

"Yes?"

"Their father died because of leprosy. He contracted it in India and never returned to live with us in our home because he was too afraid to burden us with it. When he left home years ago, Faith was yet unborn and Ethan too young to remember saying good-bye. Neither of my children had a chance to know his love. My prayer is that they will come to understand the disease so they never think of their father as simply a leper. I want them not to be ashamed of him. Or of his memory. That, I suppose, is another reason I'm here. To learn and understand. It is selfish. Getting more than I might give. But I believe we owe it to Nathaniel."

*She does not know then. She believes I am simply a patient in need of assistance.* Conflicting emotions overwhelmed Nathaniel. He wanted to rush toward her. He wanted to flee before she unwrapped his face and discovered his identity.

In the brief silence of his comprehension, she misunderstood the intensity of Nathaniel's masked gaze on her.

"You've remarried since, I'm sure," Nathaniel said. "Will your husband join you here?"

She closed her eyes slowly. Opened them. "I was engaged. But just before I was to be wed, my brother-in-law brought to me letters and diaries. Finally knowing the truth about my husband and his love for our family, I could not marry another man. That was two months ago.

"Here I go again. Burdening you with so much more than you should be forced to hear. I haven't even allowed you to sip from your tea."

He'd forgotten it. He raised it to his mouth, amazed that his hand was steady. He wondered if he could speak without a tremble in his voice.

AND IN THAT MOMENT of silence, Gabrielle burst into Nathaniel's room. Giggling. She wore a red dress. In the months since her arrival here, her hair had grown thicker and longer, well able to hold three red ribbons.

"Dadda, dadda!" She toddled toward Nathaniel, who still sat in his chair at the window. "Dadda, dadda!" She stopped at Nathaniel's knees. "Dadda?"

"What a beautiful girl," Suzanne said.

Before Nathaniel could reply, Ima stepped inside. "Where's that rascal? I should have known she would run ahead and—" Ima blinked. "Forgive me. I didn't know you had a visitor."

"No visitor," Suzanne said. "I'm Suzanne. I believe Edward discussed my arrival with you."

"And my name is Ima."

Suzanne extended a hand of greeting. Ima ignored it and hugged Suzanne before stepping back and surveying her with a smile. Life filled Ima's face. Color and joy.

"Yes," Suzanne, returning the smile. "Edward has told me all about you."

"And, yes, Edward told me you would be joining us here. May God bless all that you do as you help us here. Gabrielle and I have arrived to help this man with his bandages. But I presume now you're here for that purpose."

"Yes, I only hope I can follow the example set by you and my brother-in-law."

"Well, then," Ima said, "Gabrielle, come along. Time enough to visit later when—" Ima stopped herself.

Nathaniel watched understanding fill Ima's face.

"Brother-in-law," Ima repeated. "Edward neglected to tell me that. So Nathaniel . . ."

"Yes, Nathaniel was my husband," Suzanne said. "Edward, I'm sure, also explained the circumstances of his death."

"His death?" Ima blinked a few times, trying to understand the situation. Behind Suzanne, Nathaniel shook his head frantically and waved her away.

"There is a lot I don't know," Ima said. "But I'm sure Edward will explain it to me."

She scooped Gabrielle up and marched from the room.

SUZANNE TURNED TO NATHANIEL. "Shall we get started? I'm not a practiced nurse, but I promise to do my best."

No. Nathaniel could not allow her to unwrap his face. She had her loving memories of him. He would not destroy them by letting her see him now. How could Edward have allowed this?

She walked toward him, then paused and pointed out the window. "There are my children."

Nathaniel followed her gaze. Ethan and Faith. Running across the grass. This was too much to bear. "Tell me," he said, "would you have wished for your Nathaniel to return to you with his leprosy?"

Suzanne tucked her skirt behind her legs and sat on the edge of the bed. "Oh yes," she answered.

"But you would have seen the hideous damage done to him. I think it was wise of him not to return home."

Fierceness flashed across her face. "When I married him, I did not expect we would both be young and vigorous all our lives. When I promised before God to stay with him till death did us part, I fully expected—and prayed nightly—that he and I would grow old together. I expected that I would love him as his vision and body failed, just as he would love me no matter the ravages of time. Love grows during the difficult times, not diminishes. Nathaniel robbed me of the chance to prove my love for him, robbed me of discovering and proving how much richer our love would grow. How could you say it would have been better for him not to return?"

Did she believe this? Nathaniel wondered. Would it prove true if she actually saw him before her? Could he trust this love enough to let her unwrap his face?

"I think then," Nathaniel said, "if that is true, then he was a fool not to return."

"Yes," she said simply, "he was. I pray every day that I would have had the chance to tell him that. I still love him."

She stepped forward and reached for the bandages on Nathaniel's face. She gently pulled away the first wrap.

"Edward told me a little about you," she said quietly. "He said you were the first patient here. He said you nearly died because you had no will to live. That somehow you made it through a fever. And then you allowed Dr. Cuplinn to perform this surgery on you."

"Yes."

She pulled away the second wrap. "It sounds like a miracle," she said.

"Yes," he said. "It was."

NATHANIEL DID THINK of his vision as a miracle. Something so incredible that he'd been afraid to speak of it to anyone. He remembered his last prayer as he fell into what he knew would be his final darkness. And he remembered his fever taking him not into darkness but to a place that in his mind seemed far more real than the horrible pain of his body, to a dusty road that led into a small village of low, whitewashed buildings, to a place where he watched a small procession of men leave the village below.

"It's him!" he heard a voice behind him cry. "The Teacher! The one who heals!"

At that, Nathaniel found himself heedlessly running down the hillside, bursting forth onto the road just in front of the small procession of men.

Where Nathaniel saw him.

The gaze from those eyes pierced him, eyes that seemed to hold all truths and all sadness and all joy, eyes that saw the blackness of Nathaniel's soul and even so loved him without condition.

"If thou wilt—" Nathaniel found himself on his knees and pleading, transfixed by the man's gaze—"thou canst make me clean."

And the man spoke to Nathaniel.

"I will."

"DO YOU HAVE FAMILY?" Suzanne asked. "I've told you enough of mine."

A third strip of bandage fell to the floor.

"Yes."

"Will they visit?"

A fourth strip fell.

"I'm not sure." Nathaniel was sure of one thing. His voice had been altered by leprosy, and he had no right to expect she would recognize it. But if she saw his face when the last bandage fell away and did not know it was he, it meant Dr. Cuplinn's surgery had failed. He would say nothing and flee tonight.

A fifth strip fell. Nathaniel felt the first of the cool air against his skin.

Soon, too soon, she would see.

A sixth strip.

Nathaniel knew, too, that if she saw his face and knew it was him but flinched in revulsion, then her words of love had been a lie. He would flee in the dark of night and hide. Away from her. Again.

A seventh strip.

She was about to pull away the final strip, when he clutched her wrist. He was afraid.

"Am I hurting you?" she asked.

"No," he whispered. "Not yet."

A puzzled frown creased her face at his enigmatic remark. He let go of her wrist.

Her gentle fingers moved across his face.

Then the last strip fell away.

She gasped. "Oh dear, dear Nathaniel!" She flung herself against Nathaniel. She kissed his face. She wept tears that the skin of his face could not feel.

But it didn't matter.

They were together.

# about the author

BEST-SELLING AUTHOR Sigmund Brouwer is the author of 11 novels and several series of youth fiction, including the Tyndale releases *Out of the Shadows, Pony Express Christmas,* and the Mars Diaries. He is the cofounder of the Young Writer's Institute and travels North America to speak extensively at schools to help motivate reluctant readers.

Sigmund and his wife, recording artist Cindy Morgan, live in Red Deer, Alberta, Canada. They have a young daughter, Olivia.

# *about the artist*

A CHRISTIAN, cleverly disguised as an artist, Ron DiCianni has been a professional illustrator for nearly thirty years, commissioned by some of the world's largest companies.

In the last decade Ron has felt the inspiration to communicate godly principles through his work, considering art more communication than decoration. As a result of yielding his talent back to the Lord, he has been privileged to be in the forefront of the crusade for "Reclaiming the arts for Christ," through a Second Renaissance.

This "crusade" has included forming The MasterPeace Collection with DaySpring, conceiving and coauthoring the best-selling Tell Me series with Max Lucado, Joni Eareckson Tada, and Michael Card, as well as his solo efforts *Beyond Words* and *Travels of Messenger,* with his sons, both published by Tyndale. He has also been the cover artist for such best-selling books as *This Present Darkness, Piercing the Darkness,* and *Angelwalk.*

Most recently he has launched Art2see, a

company devoted to proclaiming Christ through a variety of artistic venues, to both the Christian and secular markets through his company's partnership with Somerset Publishing in Houston.

DiCianni and his wife, Pat, live in Buffalo Grove, Illinois. They consider their two greatest works of art to be their sons, Grant, a paramedic and firefighter, and Warren, a YWAM student currently in Perth, Australia, becoming the man of God he was born to be.

# *a note from the artist*

SIGMUND BROUWER takes the story of the leper and brings an unexpected twist that allows us to travel to a different time and place where the story once again lives on. That's truly what Scripture was meant to teach us. Specifically, it is as relevant in every age as it was when Jesus was bringing it to life.

You have no doubt often heard it said, "One picture is worth a thousand words." In the case of these novellas we decided to bring it to reality.

Each of these handsomely crafted stories is meant to bring you an experience of words and picture, which has been a lost art to many. I believe that's what Oswald Chambers alluded to when he said,

"We have lost our power to visualize. . . ."

There is a world of truth in that statement. We hope that these will set you on the road to visualize and engage the use of your imagination as you allow these stories to indelibly impact your mind

with the eternal truths of God's word. Allow yourself to dream and wonder and be immersed in the
story, because each one is about the human condition. Each one is about you.

I'm privileged to have a small part in each of
these. I hope that together the words and pictures
will remain with you forever.

*Ron DiCianni*